THE BOOK OF PASSING SHADOWS

C.V. Balakrishnan

Translated from the Malayalam original *Ayussinte Pusthakam* by

T.M. YESUDASAN

THORNBIRD
NIYOGI BOOKS

Published by
NIYOGI BOOKS
Block D, Building No. 77,
Okhla Industrial Area, Phase-I,
New Delhi-110 020, INDIA
Tel: 91-11-26816301, 26818960
Email: niyogibooks@gmail.com
Website: www.niyogibooksindia.com

Editor: Arunima Ghosh
Design: Nabanita Das
Cover design: Misha Oberoi

ISBN: 978-93-89136-82-1
Publication: 2021

Printed at: Niyogi Offset Pvt. Ltd., New Delhi, India

AUTHOR'S NOTE

I recall a night of December 1979, when I was in Calcutta on a Kerala Sahitya Akademi fellowship for the study of Bengali theatre. After watching a play by Badal Sircar in the Theosophical Society hall in College Street, I was waiting at Chowringhee for the bus to Ballygunj. Suddenly, the surrounding foggy night reverberated with the sound of music and dancing. A group of youth was seen approaching from Bentinck Street toward Chowringhee singing and dancing to the accompaniment of strings and percussion. They were singing Christmas carols. It was Christmas eve.

Memories of several forgotten Christmas festivals came flooding back. Those festivities belonged to me as well. I instinctively merged into the band of carolling youth who reminded me of those forgotten Christmases. I felt like drifting with them along the Chowringhee lane, sharing their joy and enthusiasm. It was an unforgettable experience.

A few days later, I happened to visit the famous St. Paul's Cathedral. It was daytime. The courtyard was deserted. And so was the cathedral. There was absolute silence. I took a seat in a pew facing the altar. I picked up a Bible from the desk in front, opened it, and began to read. I don't remember what I read. The only thing I remember is that I read only a little.

Then I became lost in countless memories that transported me back to another world and time. A cluster of villages lay beneath a veil of mist. Crops of ginger, turmeric, tapioca, and rubber trees covered the slopes. Four-legged watch-sheds erected by farmers dotted the countryside. Tangled webs of footpaths and rivers flowing through the woods went zigzag across the landscape. Green hills playing hide-and-seek with the rain and fog kept reappearing in the sun. The slopes were teeming with rabbits crouching in the thickets and grazing domestic swine. Wild boars were dying from biting country explosives. Church bells were chiming and pretty girls wearing scarves on their heads were hurrying to church.

Memories came crowding. The Vicar and I were playing a game of chess, our eyes glued to the chessboard. The sound of guitar and violins being practised in the adjacent room overflowed into our ears. In those days, I lived like a Christian, wearing the Catholic amulet called 'venthinga' around my neck and regularly reading the Bible. I remembered all these things sitting alone in the St. Paul's Cathedral. The idea of the novel *Ayussinte Pusthakam* germinated from these memories.

This novel began to be serialized in the weekly, *Mathrubhoomi*, from April 1983. The well known artist A.S. Nair, who drew the illustrations, once admitted to me that he was unable to represent adequately the intensity of the novel's sexuality. A girl once proudly announced that this novel was the first gift she had received from her boyfriend. A cancer patient languishing in Regional Cancer Centre,

Thiruvananthapuram, had read this book several times, before he yielded to the disease. A fellow passenger I met on a train journey confessed that this novel had helped him overcome a great crisis in his life.

Twelve years ago, *Ayussinte Pusthakam* was translated into Tamil as *Uyir Puththagam*. I am happy that a renowned publishing house like Niyogi Books is publishing an English translation of my book. I am grateful to Mini Krishnan for the steady support she has extended to make this novel accessible to a potential audience of readers of the English language.

C.V. Balakrishnan

TRANSLATOR'S NOTE

The motivation behind undertaking the translation of *Ayussinte Pusthakam* into English was circumstantial rather than personal. Sometime in 2011, when the author, C.V. Balakrishnan, visited Kottayam in connection with 30 years of its publication, friends proposed that I must translate the book into English. The author accepted the proposal and I agreed to do it, without hesitation, despite the mammoth nature of the task and the challenges of translating one of the best written novels in Malayalam. The popularity of the novel still holds even after 36 years of its publication.

Besides the initial encouragement that came from friends, my own admiration for the author and the work has equally influenced my readiness to translate *Ayussinte Pusthakam*. The ethics of translation wants us to serve the text. And the text is best served by being faithful to it. In my translation, I have tried my best to follow this principle of fidelity to the text.

Ayussinte Pusthakam deals with the trials and tribulations of a group of Catholic Christians who migrated from central Kerala and settled in north Malabar and who constituted themselves into a well-knit community of an 'edavaka' or pastorate. As such, the history of migration and settlement forms part of the substructure of the text. However, the language of the novel bears no resemblance either to the language the migrants had left behind or to the language of north Malabar where they had settled down. Though region-blind, this invented language turns out to be highly allusive and fascinating. Allusions to characters, events, and passages in the Bible, together with a well-organized plot and lucid style of writing, holds the key to the poetic function and aesthetic experience of this novel. The harmonious blend of language and theme, feeling and thought adds to the magic of the text.

The greatest challenge a translator faces is the fear of losing the original beauty of the book 'in translation'. As I set out to work on this translation, difficulties began to appear one by one. The style of language adopted by *Ayussinte Pusthakam* was modelled on the Malayalam translation of the King James Version (KJV) of the Bible. How to overcome the problem of translating the antique beauty of this biblical language back into English for contemporary readers? Thus, relying mainly on the New Revised Standard Version (NRSV) rather than the KJV, I have retained some of the characteristic biblical idioms and phrases with slight changes, for instance, 'why is your face fallen' instead of 'why has thy countenance fallen'. Another example is the use of the introducing phrase of biblical narration, 'And it came to pass'. The biblical use of the word 'know' (Gen 4:1) in the sense of 'to have sex' or 'to consummate marriage' is used in the novel several times. The proverbial saying, 'There is no witchcraft against Jacob' (Num 23:23), and the poetic phrase 'gathered to his people' (Gen 25:8) used to denote the death of a person are also suggestive of the Bible.

The tension between sexuality and spirituality and the sombre ruminations on the passing nature of human life that are corollary to the central theme of sin and retribution are suggested through allusions to passages from various books of the Bible. 'Sin lies at your door' (Gen 4:7), 'Whoever strikes father or mother shall be put to death' (Ex 21:15), and 'As for mortals, their days are like grass' (Ps 103:15) are a few examples. The archetypal or mythical scaffold lending universal significance to the novel is built on allusions lavishly drawn from the biblical books of Genesis, Exodus, Numbers, Job, Psalms, Song of Solomon, Amos, and Epistles of St. Paul.

An important historical coordinate relevant to an understanding of the novel is the Second Vatican Council of the 1960s. The question of celibacy of priests is discussed in the novel in the wake of the deliberations in this historic council.

The narrative from the beginning sets in motion a train of deaths—of Theresa, Paolo, Kochurosa, Samuel, Skaria, Yakob, and Sara. This overwhelming predominance of deaths made me translate the Malayalam title *Ayussinte Pusthakam* or the Book of Life as *The Book of Passing Shadows.*

I would like to thank Mini Krishnan for her consistent support, Latha Anantharaman, and Arunima Ghosh for their editorial attention, and Niyogi Books for publishing this book. I would also like to express my dearest wish to see *The Book of Passing Shadows / Ayussinte Pusthakam* gaining for its author a new and potential English-reading audience.

LIST OF CHARACTERS

Yohannan: the protagonist, a teenage boy
Family members: Thoma (father), Theresa (mother; passed away when Yohannan was yet a child), Annie (elder sister), Paolo (grandfather), Elisha (grandmother)

Joshi: Yohannan's classmate and closest friend
Family members: Daniel (father), Esther (mother), Susan and Valsamma (sisters)

Rahel, Silvy, Michael, Clara, Jessy, Nina*chen*:
Yohannan's schoolmates

Yakob, Philipos, Peter: Thoma's friends

Isaac: bar owner

Lohitakshan: barber

Vicar, Assistant Vicar, Ephraim, Mathew, Sister Marianos and Sister Mithiria: Members of the church in the parish

Samuel: Annie's teacher at school
Family members: Rosamma (wife) and Kochurosa (daughter)

Sara: the wife of a character called Skaria, who remains very ill throughout the novel, eventually dies, and leaves his young widow all alone, who easily becomes the object of desire for some men in the parish, and Yohannan's love interest

THE BOOK OF PASSING SHADOWS

Weeping and wailing, puffing and panting, Rahel ran. Climbing the terraces bathed in the evening shades, she reached the boundary, when she came upon Annie and Yohannan walking straight toward her. Rahel hastily wiped thc tears from her eyes and pushed on as if nothing had happened. But her heart was still crying.

Annie approached her and asked, 'Rahel, Rahel, why were you crying? Why has your face fallen?'

Fearful and trembling, Rahel ran away tearfully, letting out a pent-up cry.

Annie and Yohannan halted in fear. Soon, they followed suit, and rushed down the terraces, past the rubber trees.

Paolo tottered against the pigsty, reeling under Thoma's heavy blow. Darkness prevailed on his senses. Dragging him down on the ground, Thoma climbed onto his chest. Paolo let out a terrified scream. Thoma caught him by the throat and, tightening his grip, choked him. Writhing in pain, Paolo dug his sharp nails into Thoma's flesh. His legs beat frantically against the ground.

It was into this woeful mess that Annie and Yohannan came rushing.

Frightened, Annie called out unto the Lord for help, her palms close to her chest. Yohannan did not know what to do. He stood there for a while, deathly pale and drawn. Then he tried to pull his father away.

With a growl, Thoma pushed him and Yohannan fell on his back. Annie ran to the wagon road to see if any help was at hand.

Yohannan was badly hurt. Propping himself up on his arms and rising to his feet, he saw his grandfather naked. Yohannan quickly turned his face away.

Hearing Annie's cry for help, Yakob and Philipos ran in from the road. Together they struggled to pull Thoma away from Paolo and made him to stand aside.

'Isn't it your own father that you are battering like this?' demanded Yakob.

'An old man, too,' added Philipos.

'Even so, what should I do if he does a loathsome thing?' Thoma hissed, struggling to wriggle out of their grip.

Yakob looked at Paolo and took pity on him. He lay spreadeagled on the ground, eyes shut and groaning. Yakob bent down and covered his nakedness, putting right his dishevelled clothes.

'Why don't you ask him?' bellowed Thoma, scornfully.

'Better ask him,' said Thoma, with deep scorn.

Annie leaned on Yohannan, unable to hold back her bawl. Yohannan's slender body was overcome by shivering.

'Can't you get up?' Yakob asked Paolo, sympathetically.

Paolo was wroth and growled bitterly as he hurled blatant terms of abuse at Thoma. Once again, Thoma became a madman. Lifting his leg, he kicked Paolo and Paolo moaned. The pigs in the sty grunted too.

As Thoma prepared to kick Paolo again, Yakob and Philipos mustered all their strength and pulled him away to a safe distance.

'If only I had a dagger with me... Dammit!' Thoma cursed.

'Then you would have landed in jail for killing an old man,' said Philipos.

Smiling wryly, Thoma said, 'Who is afraid of going to jail? I have already been there once.'

Not only Yakob and Philipos, but all the parishioners remembered the incident. In those days, Paolo, the pure-hearted, went about telling them with pathos how Thoma was the first to dishonour his ancestral line by going to prison. Some of the parishioners could still clearly recall the day when Thoma went to prison. Unable to endure the humiliation, Paolo went to the churchyard and wept bitterly beside his wife Elisha's grave.

Although ripe with age, Paolo's body was not that feeble. He was shorter than Thoma. His hair was not yet entirely grey. His face was a little swollen and looked heavy. Always there was a placid and harmless air about his face. The drooping corners of his mouth may have given him this bovine look. Not in the habit of wearing a shirt, he was content with an upper cloth. His appearance and character had several of the saintly qualities, though people were hard put to define them precisely. From his early youth, he was deeply involved in church and parish activities. No one in the parish would be able to recall him missing a Holy Mass. As he advanced in years, he grew in spirit and godliness. He sanctified his old age with piety and devotion, reading regularly from the Old and New Testaments, and singing songs of praise in a crawling, subdued voice. When he chanted prayers in a trailing, mournful tone, Annie and Yohannan accompanied him, kneeling by his side, rapt in the fullness of their hearts and muttering 'Amen, Amen' at intervals.

Their pious ways were quite unfamiliar to Thoma for a fairly long time. This was not at all a secret exclusive to the family. Several God-fearing people in the parish had prophesied and warned that unless he repented and turned from sinful ways, he would perish as an unredeemable miscreant. And indeed, they all pitied his woman, Theresa.

Thoma was 30 when he took Theresa as his wife. She conceived and bore him a daughter, who was named Annie. Thoma knew his wife again. She conceived again and bore him a son. He was named Yohannan. And all the days of Theresa were forty-two years. It came to pass, when Theresa gave up her ghost, Thoma was in jail, serving a term of rigorous imprisonment for having stabbed a man. The suggestion that he be informed and released on parole to attend the funeral went unheeded before Paolo's obstinacy. Thus, Theresa was buried and was gathered to her people without Thoma ever knowing it.

Thoma heard of her death much later, from a thief.

The Thoma who returned from prison was an entirely different person. Guilt and humiliation haunted him. He was averse to going home, afraid to face his children. The thought that Theresa died while he lay fallen in some deep ditch of sin consumed him with an inconsolable grief. He took to drinking in order to forget it. And he wept bitterly whenever he remembered Theresa. He wandered listlessly in the parish, lamenting, magnifying her excellence, and confessing his own worthlessness.

Paolo was aware of Thoma's whereabouts, that he was living like a vagabond and wandering like a fugitive, refusing to accept solace from anyone. But he affected ignorance and never betrayed himself. When someone told him that Thoma used to sleep in the cemetery at night, he answered with an indifferent grumble.

Then one day, an astonishing thing happened.

Paolo had just come back from church after the Sunday service. The fragrance of frankincense from the censer at the Holy Mass still lingered about him. Spiritual admonitions such as 'Let everything be done in brotherly love' and 'Salute one another with a holy kiss' still echoed in his mind. He lay on the veranda couch and dozed off, for how long he did not know. Feeling a wetness under his feet, he woke up. His feet were sweating profusely as a forewarning, a premonition. As he opened his eyes, he saw Thoma, who bowed, fell on his father's feet, kissed them, and asked forgiveness for all his sins and transgressions. On seeing Thoma like this, Paolo was overwhelmed with emotion. He crossed himself, remembering the grace and commandments of God, the Creator, with deep gratitude. Pressing his face against his son's forehead, he broke down and wept, 'My God, my God!'

What befell the house that used to observe feasts with the unleavened bread of sincerity and sanctity? What happened to Thoma, who by repentance had removed the thorn in his flesh and washed himself clean of all his sins? What was the secret that made him kick his father indiscriminately like a domestic pig? Where did he find this wine of wrath?

It all appeared to be a mystery to Yakob. He looked suspiciously at Thoma.

Yohannan looked at his father with revulsion. Annie grew pale in fear.

Thoma stood seething with anger. Intent on probing the mystery, Yakob, approached him tactfully.

'What will be shall be, so goes the saying. But I think there is a reason for everything, especially for a son to kick his father.'

'It is none of your business.'

'Don't be so pigheaded. This is not a petty thing.'

'Hmm!' Thoma said furiously, 'Then go and fetch the police.'

Hearing this, Yakob recoiled and retreated, shrugging his shoulders.

'If calling the police will settle the problem, we will do as you wish,' said Philipos. 'But that does not suffice. There is more to it than what meets the eye.' He drew very close to Thoma. 'We've known each other for many years, haven't we? I can see that your mind is greatly troubled. You seem to think that you are trapped in a blind alley. There is a way out of everything. After all, we are all members of the same parish and worship in the same church, don't we?'

'What of that?' responded Thoma.

Philipos answered, 'You do not know what you have done. You and your family have a good name in the parish. And in one day, everything…'

Philipos went on speaking. But Thoma did not hear him. His soul wept. He leaned against a pillar lest he should fall. He stood there like a sickly child, with his arms clasped behind his head.

Closely observing him, Yakob concluded that he was in the grip of a severe mental shock. But he could also feel a sense of aversion, because Thoma stood there like a closed book of undeciphered symbols.

'Thoma*cha*, please speak to me.' Obviously, Philipos was losing his patience.

'Get lost, I say. Go away and poke your nose elsewhere.'

'That is fine! Elsewhere! Nothing more important has happened in this parish today, or even anywhere else. Sons might have beaten their fathers before. It may happen in the future also. But your beating your father is quite different. Where shall we go without knowing the truth? How can we go in peace without knowing it?'

'Then, for God's sake, don't take the trouble of leaving,' muttered Thoma.

Philipos turned to Yakob and said, 'We are in a fix, aren't we?'

'True.'

Then Philipos turned to the children and said, 'Children, do you know anything?'

Hugging Yohannan close to her, Annie shook her head.

Thoma gestured his children to go inside the house. They stepped onto the veranda and stood uncertain by the door. Above them, on the lintel, hung a crucifix.

Then, quite unexpectedly, Paolo buried his face in the ground and wept. Yakob approached him and said, 'Don't cry.'

But Paolo wept sore. His body trembled, and his elbows were bleeding.

'You can't lie here like this any longer. Come on, get up, will you?' Yakob said, taking Paolo's hand.

'No, no,' Paolo resisted.

But Yakob insisted.

Even with Yakob's support, Paolo struggled to get up. He sat up, moaning and groaning. Slapping the dust from

Paolo's hair and aching back, Yakob thought, there is no cause to believe that Thoma would beat up this fellow without sufficient reason. We have never heard of Thoma beating his father even in those reckless days when he was a headstrong young man picking fights and playing cards.

Paolo inspected his elbows.

'Hurt, are you?' Yakob asked.

'Yes.'

'Let me see, where?'

'Ow,' Paolo groaned in pain.

'It is nothing serious. Only a scrape. There is nothing to worry about. Get up. Go inside and lie down.' Yakob helped him to his feet.

When he started to walk, Philipos said, 'Until yesterday, you were more than a father and son to each other, bound by love. Last Friday, in the front yard of the church, I heard you with my own ears telling Puthiyapurel Devassi that Thoma was loving and more than just a son. *Chettan*, at least you tell us what happened. Why did Thoma*chen*...'

'It is nothing, nothing at all.' Paolo said, averting his face.

'So, Thoma*chen* kicked you just like that for no reason?' asked Philipos. 'Then we must sound the alarm bell and inform all the parishioners. A son who smites his father should be put to death. That is what Moses heard from Jehovah, isn't it?'

Thoma glared at him.

'It was not without any reason.' His voice quivered. 'I will tell...'

Then he began to describe his father's sin.

Thoma got up and started walking, not knowing exactly where he was going. Finally, he stopped in front of Isaac's pub.

'A-ha, I feared *Chettan* had forgotten his way here,' said Isaac as he wiped the bench clean with a cloth. Thoma did not take that seat. Instead, he sought a dark corner in the lean-to behind the room.

Even at first glance, it occurred to Isaac that Thoma's fallen face reflected some deep anguish. He sprang to action and filled a glass with arrack.

'Good. *Chettan*, drink this first, and deal with everything else later.'

Thoma avidly poured it into his throat.

'Some more, please.'

Isaac managed a light smile.

'I had a hunch you wouldn't stop with that. You have abstained from it and stayed away from here for a very long time, haven't you?'

Isaac brought another glass of arrack mixed with *arishtam* (a fermented decoction) and a plate of fried pork. Then he thought of keeping him company, considering that Thoma should not be sitting there alone. He poured a drink for himself and took a seat beside Thoma's plate of pork.

'To be honest, there is no one like Thoma*chettan* in the whole neighborhood who knows the art of drinking. You may wonder why I am saying this. You are not one of the general run of wine-bibbers. Of course, there are men who walk away with steady steps after drinking 600 or 700 milli of arrack. That is a different matter. But *Chettan* is a type apart. See, for example. It has been a long time since *Chettan* stopped coming here. And today you have come without any prodding. You know the true worth of arrack. It has been something you drink when you want it. That is my point. You abstained from it when you did not feel the need. Today, you have come, thinking that you cannot do without it.' Isaac swallowed a gulp. Then, putting two morsels of pork into his mouth, he started speaking about the quality of that day's pork.

Isaac was given to speaking at length on any silly matter. Thoma sat there with his eyes fixed on Isaac's face, pretending to pay close attention to what he was saying. Isaac had no other customers to attend to. Realizing that the quality of pork was not an interesting subject, he shifted to a news item he had come across in the paper. It was about a eugenics project to collect and distribute the sperm of eminent scholars and scientists. Thoma did not utter a single word.

There were voices outside. Isaac rose from his seat and said, 'I suppose I should go and take a look.'

It was Yakob and Philipos. Yakob peeped into the room through the slit in the blue curtain. The room was empty. Just then, Isaac appeared.

'Yakob*chettan*, why do you stop there? Why don't you come in?' Isaac complained.

Isaac knew that Yakob, who was in the habit of home-brewing, did not need his services. Though Yakob made liquor for his own use and did not sell it, home-brewing was still a crime. But if complaints were made against him, no action would follow; there was, as the proverb says, no sorcery against Yakob.

'Did Thoma*chen* come this way?' enquired Yakob.

'No.' Isaac shook his head.

Yakob and Philipos entered the room.

'Where else would he go?' Philipos took a step towards Isaac.

When it was clear that he would find Thoma in the lean-to, Isaac confessed to Yakob, 'Yes, he is sitting over there.'

'Why this hide and seek?' Yakob asked roughly.

Isaac clarified his position. 'He came here greatly troubled by something. I thought no one should disturb him.'

By this time, Philipos had found Thoma in the dark corner of the lean-to. Yakob followed him. When Thoma saw them, everything he had tried to forget seemed to return. He wished they had not followed him to the pub. He sat there on the floor in deep shame. But soon he wanted to know what they thought about what he had done to his father. How would they react if they were in his place?

'I am happy that you two are here. Otherwise, by our Lord, I would have come seeking you.' He said this with all sincerity.

Flattered by this reception, they sat on the floor in front of Thoma. Yakob strictly forbade Isaac from admitting anyone into the lean-to.

Isaac agreed.

'Now, don't loiter here. We will call you if necessary.'

'Right.'

Yakob poured arrack evenly into the glasses. He emptied his glass in a single pull. Philipos wiped his mouth uncomfortably and searched his pocket in vain for the packet of beedi. Yakob offered him a cigarette.

'Thoma*chettan*, you also take one,' Yakob said. Thoma did not refuse. As he put it between his lips, Philipos lit it.

Yakob was quite ready for a discussion, felt Thoma. But he did not know what Philipos thought.

'By the by, Thoma*chettan* said a little while ago that you would have come seeking us if we had not turned up here.' Keeping his tone light, Yakob started to speak in a matter-of-fact manner. 'You want to tell us something, don't you?'

'Yes.'

Thoma looked up startled. He reached for Yakob's right hand and held it tight. Then, looking plaintively into his eyes, he asked, 'Are you saying that I am guilty? Tell me, frankly. I am burning within.'

Yakob was deeply touched, when Thoma, whom he considered a better person than himself in all respects, took his hand in a humble manner and made a request in a faltering voice. He did not know what to say. He turned to Philipos for some hint. But Philipos was absorbed in smoking his cigarette, and Yakob looked to himself for the right response.

'Just now it occurred to me,' he uttered every word with care and precision, 'what Thoma*chettan* has done is forbidden.'

When he heard this, Thoma was greatly disappointed. He hastily withdrew his hand from Yakob's and bent his head as if he was doomed.

Yakob suddenly added, 'But as I think it over, I wonder whether what the old man did was right.'

Yakob was impressed by his own way of dealing with this complicated problem. He had rehearsed it in advance.

'Sin lies at your door. It is staring at you. You must control it. We have learnt this from the Scriptures, haven't we? We have also heard stories of how God destroyed the sinners and their cities.' He said all this in the deep, commanding voice of an evangelist. 'Who are we to judge the sinners? All are sinners, says the Holy Book.'

Meanwhile, Philipos wondered how Yakob had acquired such eloquence. But it did not seem so exceptional to Thoma, who was in a broken state.

'But,' Yakob continued, 'what we should examine here is whether something we can call "a sinful act" has occurred.'

Yakob took a break to take a bite of the pork and a sip of the arrack. Thoma followed suit. But Philipos remained absorbed in his cigarette.

'In my view, the old man may be around 70 or 75. That daughter of George is barely 12 or 13 years. Does his behaviour cause any suspicion? Can't it be an act of pure, sublime love?' Yakob paused, though he did not expect a reply.

Thoma's lips moved. 'When I reached the house, I saw Rahel struggling to wriggle out of that fellow's grip. But when he saw me, his grip slackened, and she tore away. She ran away, sobbing. She glanced at me before she ran. The pain in her eyes! I have never seen so much pain in my life.'

In this confession, Thoma laid down all his troubles and sorrows before them. In the weariness that followed the confession and the casting away of a burden, he lifted up his glass with a sigh and found that it was empty.

'I want some more,' he told Philipos.

Philipos retched.

'We are drunk already,' Philipos said a little ruefully.

'It doesn't matter if I come come a little undone, today. It is the day on which sin fell upon me as well.' Saying this, Thoma broke down and wept desperately and uncontrollably, as if he were alone and desolate. Yakob and Philipos were deeply touched and pained by Thoma's passionate cry. They sought ways to console him.

'Come, let's go home. I'll go with you to the door,' said Philipos.

'Going home? Nothing doing.' Thoma grew pale as if he had heard something very dreadful.

'Won't the little ones wait for you there?'

'Yes.' He heaved a long sigh. 'They will wait. Still, I am not going there now.'

He thought of his children. He remembered pushing Yohannan down when he tried to pull him away with his tender hands. He remembered Annie shuddering with sobs.

It was then that he thought of the brimstone and fire that had fallen on his house. The little ones will know this. Perhaps they have already learnt about it. They may have heard everything he said to Yakob and Philipos on the spot. They will tremble with shame and humiliation when they know what their grandfather did to Rahel. Children will deride them at school. The shadow of sin will fall upon them also. Woe, woe, woe unto me!

'Then, you are welcome to spend the night with us at my house,' suggested Philipos.

Thoma rose to his feet as if he had made up his mind. His steps were faltering. He plodded on toward Isaac. There were several men sitting on the bench and the floor. He did not recognize any of them.

'Pour me one more drink and tell me how much for the three of us.'

'Enough for today,' Philipos remonstrated.

'No, I am all right. Isaac knows it well.'

Isaac was in a dilemma.

'Hey, pour me one more drink, I say.'

Isaac obeyed.

Thoma took a sheaf of rupee notes from his pocket and began to count them.

'Now tell me, how much?'

Isaac calculated the amount.

'For all of us, do you hear?'

'Yes.'

'Thoma*chettan*, don't pay our bill,' Yakob said.

'Shut up, will you? I want to pay. Or else, I will feel bad.'

'*Chettan*, do as you please.'

Outside, it was coal dark. Not one of them could tell what time it was.

'You two go on. I would like to be alone for a while.'

'Where shall we go leaving you alone in this condition?' asked Philipos.

'Go, I say. Your wife and children are waiting for you. Go away. My woman, my children's mother, is there....' He pointed northward to the darkened hilltop. 'She is there. I must go to her in the cemetery...'

'*Ayyo*! You should not go there now, Thoma*cha*. It is dark,' Philipos, worried, tried to warn him.

'Don't go there,' Yakob cautioned him against it as well.

'I am going there, no matter what you say. There is enough sense left in me. Leave me alone. Go away.'

Then Thoma disappeared into the night. He fumbled and stumbled along the road to the church. More than once, he fell on his knees and got up again, groaning. He did not feel the blood dripping from his wounded knees. Far away, the foxes howled. Every now and again, he quite unintentionally lifted up his eyes to the heavens, which looked as white as a shroud.

Entering the cemetery, he looked for the grave of his dearly beloved Theresa. He stumbled on a cross and fell on the ground. Weary from weeping and wailing, he fell asleep.

The earth wailed. The heavens above darkened. There was no lamp on the veranda. Yohannan was in the kitchen with Annie. Whenever the fire in the hearth began to die, one of them poked the firewood a little to keep it alive. Thoma stood outside silently for a long time, watching the fire burn. When Yohannan began to nod off, Annie said to him, 'Have your supper and go to bed.'

She served him some leftover rice and dried-fish curry.

'Did Grandpa eat?' Yohannan asked.

A shot was heard from the riverbank. She looked at Yohannan with fright. He understood her frightened look. Some poachers were out hunting a tusker.

'*Chechi*, you also come with me.'

'No, I'm not hungry.'

'Then, I will eat only after Grandpa has eaten.'

'Go and fetch him then.'

'*Chechi* also come with me.'

Yohannan marched in the front, carrying the kerosene lamp. He was seized by an irrational fear as he stepped out into the veranda. Annie held on to his shoulder. On the coir bed set across the southern part of the veranda, Paolo lay wrapped from head to foot in a blanket; he was shivering, as if infected with typhoid. Drawing near, Yohannan called him.

He pulled the blanket from his face. He looked at them with the pathos of a dying man. His face was swollen from the beating. His eyes seemed too small to be seen.

After looking at them sorrowfully for a while, he said in a faltering voice, 'Children, you may go.'

As they turned and walked back, they heard heaving sobs from the darkness behind them. Yohannan involuntarily caught hold of a corner of Annie's skirt in fear. When he sat down again for supper, he felt no appetite at all.

'What are you thinking? The food is getting cold,' said Annie.

'*Chechi*, don't you remember the day our mother died? That evening…' His voice dropped to a whisper.

'Please eat your rice instead of thinking this and that.'

'*Chechi*, you also eat.'

They ate from the same plate as they used to when they were little. Their hands moved mechanically, and they were silent till the plate was empty. The only sound in the dead silence came from the jingle of Annie's bangles.

Yohannan was sleepless. The lamp was left on in the corner, its flame lowered. Annie lay on her side facing the wall.

'*Chechi*.'

She was mum.

Yohannan wanted to know something, but hesitated to ask. He lay for a while, thinking.

'*Chechi*,' he again called.

'Yes?'

'Are you asleep?'

'No.'

Again, he hesitated.

'What do you want?'

'It's nothing.'

Some time passed.

'*Chechi*, what did Grandpa do to Rahel?' he asked.

Annie did not answer. She too had been wondering the same thing.

Rahel was not sleeping. All the others were asleep after snuffing out the lamp. Shiny and Silvy slept nearby, snoring loudly in turns. The conversation between father and mother in the next room had died down. They too had fallen asleep. Rahel alone could not sleep.

Rahel scraped her palm roughly against the bricks on the wall. Her burning sighs fell upon the wall. She puffed and panted like a young rabbit that has escaped from the hunter. Her tears spilled over her cheeks in the dark. She bit her fingers in order to control her sobs. Never in her life had she felt such an agonizing pain.

Rahel had gone to the house just to see Annie. Nibbling a lemon leaf, she ran onto the veranda, calling 'Annie!'

'She and the boy are gone somewhere,' said Paolo, who sat on the coir bed unrolling a beedi.

'Where did they go?'

'A-a-a-a!' he shrugged.

'Then I am leaving. I'll come later.'

Rahel was about to step down from the veranda when he said, 'Wait, they'll be back soon. They left long ago. Are you in a hurry, my child?'

'Not at all.'

'Then sit here. I am quite bored sitting alone.'

'All right, Grandpa, I'll keep you company.' With a smile Rahel sat on the bench by the table.

Annie and Yohannan's books were piled on the table. Tucked into them was a weekly, which she pulled out to read. She decided to read the serial until Annie returned.

'Grandpa, what are you doing?'

'Rolling a beedi.'

Rahel could not suppress her laughter.

'Is rolling beedi a thing to do at your age?'

He giggled for some time. Then he blew away the tobacco from the unrolled beedi leaf. Rahel watched him closely.

'Do you know, my child, that old age is hell?' It was quite obvious that he said it sorrowfully.

'Why, Grandpa?'

'Here there are Thoma*chen* and his children. Still, how lonely I am!' There was a startling pathos in his words. 'To be alone is like being dead; a dead man though living!'

He was overtaken by a sudden wave of self-contempt.

'I am fed up with this life. No one understands me. They will understand when they themselves become old and alone like this.'

His voice dropped lower and lower and trailed off. For a while, he did not utter any word, but sat gazing on the floor. Rahel felt pity for him.

He picked up a paper packet from under the bed and opened it. His fingers trembled with the cares of solitude.

'Oh, only seeds!' he muttered.

'What is that?' Rahel enquired.

When she came near, with an impish smile, he lifted the packet to her face. It had a pungent smell. It was hemp.

'That barber boy gave me this. You cannot trust him. He has neither integrity nor truth. He charged two rupees for this.' He cursed the barber, Lohitakshan. Rahel took the packet from his hands and started to remove the seeds. She did not know how to console a lonely old man, but she thought it a good thing to be of some help to him in this way.

'Oh, why do you fill this in your beedi? You will get a pain in your chest.'

'Ha, ha... What if I get a chest pain at this age? I was 73 last Passover. Child, do you know when I will feel the happiest?'

'When?' asked Rahel.

'When I see my grave in the cemetery,' he giggled.

Rahel looked sadly at his face.

'Grandpa will live to see many more Passovers.'

'Excellent!' Her words fired his enthusiasm. 'Though I don't wish for it, it is very sweet of you to say it,' he said, affectionately caressing her hair.

She laughed. She turned her attention again to the packet of hemp. His fingers kept caressing her hair. She was quite unmindful of it.

But, all of a sudden, something happened, something loathsome. Rahel wept as she remembered it.

Paolo too was awake and weeping silently in the dark. His bones burned in the fire of guilt. He imagined, he was lying in the depth of a boar pit. All the people stood along the mouth of the pit and mocked him. They were the same people who had once smothered him with love and respect. He deserved it, he thought. He was filled with bitterness. It felt like frogs were leaping onto his body. They have been assigned by God unto this parish, unto this house, unto this bedspread…

In an instant, in a second, everything crumbled. Paolo recoiled into himself. He felt feverish and the taste of blood in his mouth. How fierce it is to drift about, helpless as a worm in the endless quagmire where all filth sediments! How terrible it is to lose divine grace and fall into the ditch! How—but suddenly, two hands lifted him up. A lock of hair, as soft as silk, caressed him on the cheek—an angel.

Lord! An angel comes and touches me. She takes my hand that are loath to touch. An angel... No, I just thought about the girl, Rahel. I cannot believe it myself. But this is what actually happened. She was lifting me up from the humiliation I suffered, and from the miry clay I wallowed in. Once again, I became a sinner. But is there anyone who is not a sinner? We all are sinners... Sometimes, it may be a sinful act that makes life meaningful. For me, it was such a moment. Then I knew once again the smell of earth and green leaves. I felt the warmth of the morning sun. It was not the girl Rahel—daughter of George, the sawyer—who stood close in front of me. It was a wonder. Some change had occurred in me from the very moment she arrived. I was lonely and she offered to keep me company. I thought I must confess everything to her—about the sorrow and perplexity of old age. And when she heard it, yes, she felt pity. There was sympathy and sadness on her face. When she said that I would see many more Passovers, I was thrilled as if I had heard my Elisha's voice. I remembered the Passover days I had spent with Elisha. Rahel was smiling. There was a bloom on her cheek. I found it invigorating. The fringe of her blue skirt brushed against my knee. My veins came alive, like the streams flowing from the hills in the nascent spring rain. I felt tender leaves sprouting in my heart. Her hair was as soft as silk. I slowly ran my fingers through it. She acquiesced. Her body had an enticing scent, like black pepper or cardamom. Touching and caressing, my heart became eager to know her body...

Oh! Paolo groaned. Instead of trying to purify himself by confessing the sin and praying for forgiveness, he was indulging in memories. He felt utter self-contempt, when he realized this. The swellings were still there on his body, the marks of Thoma's kicks and blows. What Thoma did was not wickedness, but justice. He ran toward me with a roar. He caught me and pushed me out. The rest I don't remember. In my anger, I kicked him back. When he dragged me onto the ground and tried to choke me, I scratched him. I perpetrated one wrong after another. The news will spread in the parish. All the parishioners will know this. When the police arrested Thoma*chen* for getting into some petty skirmish, I wept and wailed and accused him of disgracing our family. And now what have I done? How miserable Annie and Yohannan will feel when they know this. They will never forget this. They will never remember their grandfather with affection. They will never forgive me. No one in the parish will ever consider Paolo as a person worth remembering. The elderly will never mention my name in front of their children. Girls in scarves on their way to scripture lessons will tremble when they hear my name. The drunks will sing about me. I am no longer a man, but a vermin, an object of humiliation, a butt of ridicule…

'Enough!' Paolo was surprised. Whose voice was this? He stared bewildered into the pitch black. Someone stood in the darkness pointing his finger at him. 'Get up, let me warn you, if you lie here curled like this, pondering, soon the night will pass.'

Paolo leaped to his feet and followed the unknown voice. Night sounds fell upon his ears. Lightning flashed in the east above the woods and hills. He walked laboriously and with unsteady steps. Walking past the rubber trees, he called to mind delightful memories of the past. A dry and painful smile stretched across his lips for a short while.

All these rubber trees are familiar to me. I planted them with my own hands. Like Noah who first ploughed the soil, I laboured on this land. I came here every day to see the tender leaves sprouting on the plants rooted deep in the red soil. The leaves would be wet from the dew that had rained in the night. When I trod on this earth, I heard a soft scraping. I knew this earth as intimately as I knew Elisha's body. I knew where a touch would excite this earth to rise in passion, bubbling with laughter.

Paolo saw the church on the hilltop in the north. He knelt on the ground and crossed himself.

A cold gust of wind hit the old man immersed in prayer. He trembled from head to foot. He was poured out like water. All his bones were out of joint. His heart was like wax, melted in the midst of his bowels. His strength was dried up like a potsherd. His tongue cleaved to the roof of his mouth. He was brought into the dust of death.

He did not know how long he stood there. He burst into tears. 'Have mercy on me, have mercy on me...' he cried.

In the end, he rose and went about searching for a strong branch. He found a tree that he had never planted. He scrambled up its trunk. He made acquaintance with its bark and leaves, and reached the top.

The tree was covered in darkness. As he hung like a leaf from the branch, a deep sleep fell upon him. And he was gathered to his people.

Yohannan opened his eyes. Whenever he woke up from a nap in this coir bed, the first thing that caught his eye was a pair of old leather slippers. Those slippers, which once lay under the bed, were one day thrown away somewhere by his father. It remained a mystery how, after two days, they got a perch up there on the beam above the pillar. He asked Annie. She did not know. He did not have the courage to ask his father. Although a little out of place up there, those leather slippers continued to be a property of the house. It seemed that they would be there forever, even after the leather frayed and the nails rusted.

Reading his grandfather's Bible, Yohannan lay on his back on the coir bed, intending not to sleep. But he did not realize when sleep came to him. In his slumber, he heard many voices and saw several visions. 'You are dust and unto dust shall you return'; aprons made of fig leaves sewed together; firstlings of sheep; cry from the field; springs of water; gates of water opening wide; a green olive branch; altar for burnt offerings; tents; 'Look now toward heaven, and tell the stars if you are able to number them'; 'the heat of the sun in the plains of Mamre'; 'Sarah laughing by the tent door'; 'You did laugh'; 'a pillar of salt'; 'asses bridled';

'camels at the well of water'; 'a coat of many colours'; cattle; Exodus.

Tired from seeing and hearing so many things, his eyes ached, and he woke up. For some time, he struggled to keep his eyes open. He looked at his face in the mirror. His eyes were red. He slowly ran his fingers above his upper lip. Though they were not markedly visible, he could feel the soft downy hairs. When he ran his fingers over them, he felt them rise. The vast pastures of the evening sun were spread across the valleys outside.

Yohannan stepped out. Annie called out to him, 'Where are you going?'

'Just out.'

'Come back soon, will you?'

'I will.'

The holidays were going on. When school was in session, classes would take up Yohannan's time until the evening. If he strolled around for some time after school, it would get dark by the time he got back home. When he would finally fall asleep, night would have waned.

Annie's school final exams were over. No matter what the results were, she was not likely to continue her studies. She was sure to pass, probably with a first class. But that did not matter. The college was far away in the town. She could study there, only if she stayed in the convent. But her father did not like the idea. He wanted her to look after the housework. 'I cannot bother to marry again,' he had recently declared.

Yohannan picked up a branch from the road and poked the bush on the roadside. In the bush, he heard some movement—a rabbit?

In Baby's house, there is a cage full of rabbits. It was his elder brother, Nina*chen*, who had built the cage and started the rabbit farm. It is very interesting to watch rabbits running about in the yard. 'Do you know how easy it is to kill a rabbit?' Baby asked Yohannan one day.

Every Sunday, an ox or a pig was slaughtered behind Lazar's shop. After skinning and slicing the animals, he distributed the meat among the parishioners in packets made of leaves. Lazar's daughter, Mary, was Annie's classmate. She also sat for the exam, but was likely to fail. Unfortunately, she hardly got any time to read and write. She always had a heavy load of work. In the evenings, she could be seen on the riverbank, grazing the buffaloes. Her body would glisten like oozing oil.

While walking through the woods, he came to a turning, when he saw Rahel and Silvy coming straight. They were coming from the grocer's shop. Silvy had a bottle of cooking oil in her hand.

Yohannan passed them without raising his head. His mind became restless and disturbed whenever he saw Rahel.

The previous year, Rahel was in his class, but he seldom spoke to her. Generally, he was shy with the girls. His face flushed red when girls approached him to borrow a pen or a notebook. And when they stretched their hands out to return them, he would not look them in the face.

He sighed with relief, when Rahel passed by him. He thought, however much I try, I don't understand what Grandfather tried to do to this slip of a girl. She never visited our house after that incident. It seems nobody outside our circle has heard about it. Yakob*chettan* and Philipos*chettan* might be keeping it a closely guarded secret. Shame! If it falls on the ears of fellows like Michael, it will create a huge uproar in the school. Thank God, nobody knows. That is why she is able to attend school without any embarrassment. Or do they know everything and keep mum, fearing the consequences and thinking of the horror of the sin?

Then Yohannan seemed to hear the voice of his grandfather reading the verses: 'In the beginning, God created the heaven and the earth. And the earth was without form, and void; and darkness was upon the face of the deep. And the spirit of God moved upon the face of the waters. And God said, let there be light; and there was light. And God saw that it was good. And God divided the light from the darkness. And God called the light day and the darkness he called night. And the evening and the morning were the first day.'

A lively game was in progress in the volleyball court. The spectators shouted at the top of their voices when *Kochachen* (the Assistant Vicar) placed the ball with precision in the undefended gaps in the opposite court. It was said that *Kochachen* was a brilliant volleyball player even as a schoolboy. After watching the scramble in the court and the volleys of the ball for some time, Yohannan became bored. He walked toward the church. Two nuns came straight down the steps, talking and laughing about something. The two of them, white as snow, were Sister Mithria and Sister Marianos. Yohannan stood there filled with wonder, until they reached the ground and disappeared.

And it came to pass, he walked toward the cemetery. He trod carefully among the graves. This was a world apart. The dead sleep in their graves under the shadow of the crosses. All the days of a man are but a shadow, says the Bible.

Yohannan stood silently beside his mother, Theresa's grave.

There is hope for a tree. If it is cut down, it will sprout again, and new shoots will appear on it. Though its roots grow old in the earth and its stump dies in the ground, it buds and puts forth branches, like a young plant at the scent of water. But where does a man go after he dies?

A face glowing with love and a compassionate smile lit up his memory. A childhood memory came to his mind, of lying on his mother's shoulder as she walked downhill after a holy mass in the church. He couldn't recall how old he was then. Still, the sight he saw at that time was vivid in his memory. He remembered even the shape of the pebbles he saw then lying on the road. And he had many times recaptured that sight in his dreams. Perhaps, it was only a dream—a dream in an afternoon nap or in the night.

When he came out of the cemetery, he saw the Vicar and Ephraim talking in front of the church. Ephraim is the Vicar's cook. But he is more than just a cook to the priest. Ephraim has a heart full of love and innocence. Ephraim called him, probably prompted by the Vicar. Yohannan went to them.

'Were you alone in the cemetery?'

'Yes.'

The Vicar affectionately placed his hand on his shoulder. The priest's hands were cold. Yohannan gazed into the compassionate eyes behind the spectacles. There was pathos in his eyes.

'What is troubling you, son?'

'It's nothing.'

He dropped his eyes.

'Where is Thoma*chen*? He is hardly seen nowadays.'

'He went to the hills.'

'He has some land there,' Ephraim reminded the priest.

'O, then that is it. I thought…' He seemed relieved.

'You and Annie are alone at home, aren't you?' enquired Ephraim.

'Yes.'

'When will Thoma*chen* return?'

'He did not tell us.'

'You must read and study, even if it is vacation. Don't waste your time wandering about,' the Vicar counselled him.

'Yes.'

'It seems like it is going to rain,' said Ephraim.

'Will it?' The priest looked at the sky. 'Yes, then go on, Yohannan.'

Looking once again at the Vicar's face, Yohannan went down the slope.

The gravel road led to the riverbank. It began to rain before Yohannan reached the riverside. Waking from a protracted sleep, the earth said blissfully to the first falling drops, 'Oh, you have come!' The polite voice of custom, the scent of unleavened bread!

Yohannan did not enter the watch-house built on stilts among the rocks. He longed for the rain. He kept walking unhurriedly through the shower. It would be fascinating to watch it rain on the river, he thought.

The grass that had survived even the summer heat had turned yellow.

The rocks were darkened.

The bushes were more yellow than green.

Shivering in the wind, Yohannan stood looking at the river, his hands clasped on his chest. The rain danced before him like a skein of delicate threads. He walked on, receiving the rain on his hair, on his forehead, and cheeks.

The earth was soaking in the rain. He raised his eyes when he heard the cry of buffaloes from under the *anjili* or the wild jack tree. They were Lazar*chettan*'s buffaloes. Perhaps Mary had not come to drive them home. Or she might have gone home or to the shop, leaving them to graze.

As he went a few steps, he heard someone speaking in a smothered voice. He looked around startled. He realized that the sound came from behind the bush on his right. He stepped slowly and carefully toward the bush and crouched behind the leaves.

His eyes opened wide with amazement. On the other side, Nina*chen* and Mary were cuddling each other on the wet grass. Mary began to laugh, turning her face toward the sky. Raindrops fell upon her face. Her hair, unbound, lay scattered over the leaves and grass. Running his fingers through her hair, Nina*chen* brought his face close to hers. When he raised his face again, she laughed. He pressed his lips upon her cheeks and lips. Yohannan's body began to shiver. His lips and hands trembled uncontrollably. His heart beat faster. Mary had taken off her blouse. Yohannan's eyes fell faltering on her little breasts. Mary covered her eyes with her palms. Transparent drops of rain fell on her light skin, on her soft and supple breasts, and upon her taut nipples. Nina*chen*'s face suddenly obscured them. Mary clutched her arms tightly around Nina*chen*'s back. They became locked in a passionate embrace, fusing into a single body. Yohannan sat speechless, stunned. He could not move, even though he wanted to leave. He was afraid his gasps and agitation could be heard on the other side of the bower. He turned his face away in fear. But he could not subdue his eagerness. Naked limbs were writhing in pleasure. Nina*chen* showered Mary with kisses. He nibbled at her cheeks and the nape of her neck, babbling. Moaning, Mary swayed her head from side to side. Perplexed, Yohannan withdrew his eyes once again. He felt his body overwhelmed by something. He darted his eyes again toward the lovers. Mary sat up, wiping the rain from her face and pushing away wet and sticky stray hairs. And it came to pass that Yohannan clearly saw her breasts. While he eagerly watched them, wishing to see more, she put on her blouse and covered them. Then she tied back her hair.

Mary wiped her face again. Flashing a wan smile and looking around warily, Nina*chen* hurried away. Mary was not smiling. There was fear writ on her face. She stood up, shook the dirt and grass from her skirt, and walked toward the buffaloes, looking around nervously.

In order to avoid being seen by her, Yohannan tried to leave without making a sound. But alas, the leaves underneath his feet rustled, and Mary turned toward him, frightened.

She saw Yohannan. He did not know what to do. He stood there for a while, caught in a dilemma. He wanted to run away. He ran along the wet ground, pretending not to see her. He did not look back, though she called out to him. She stood there, feeling exposed and helpless.

As he lay down to sleep at night, a white dove descended upon him. Its flapping wings rubbed him all over. In the heat of the chafing wings, he touched his own body, which trembled like a leaf. His body was in ecstasy, crooning its own melodies. The dove continued to flap its wings. His body was quickened and became nervous; it was the first time.

The parishioners were leaving after the holy mass. It was Samuel Sir, who noticed at the doorstep that Annie had been crying during the service.

What happened to Annie, he wondered. He liked her very much. At school, she sat in the classroom at the right end of the back bench. Eyes wide open, she picked up every word he said. Annie always reminded him of his own daughter, Kochurosa, who died one summer, leaving him and his wife, Rosamma, alone. May her soul rest in peace…

What Samuel Sir found in Annie were his daughter's eyes. While reading out the Bible to Kochurosa at night, he frequently used to look at her face. Her eyes seemed always open, riveted on his face. They would gleam with unshed tears, if she heard something sad being read out. He used to take her along for evening walks. Kochurosa's cheeks would receive fondling caresses from innumerable hands as they walked along, making casual enquiries and exchanging greetings with acquaintances. 'Is Rosa*mol* taking a walk with papa?'; 'Sir, we won't let you go without drinking coffee'; 'Sir, you may go. We will bring her home after a little while'; 'No money from you for this bottle of honey, sir. It is for Kochurosa, free of charge.'

Samuel Sir could not control himself, when he remembered all these things. He would lift his eyes to the heavens in the hope of seeing her flying across the clouds. Then deep sighs, tempest-like, would fill his heart.

The parishioners often regretted that God showed no mercy to Samuel Sir, who had voluntarily undergone a vasectomy after the doctors warned strictly against a second pregnancy for Rosamma. Was it right to plunge such a God-fearing family into darkness in this way?

Samuel Sir and Rosamma never denounced the church, even after Kochurosa's death. They sought the Lord as if they had no other refuge. They always praised Him. They attended the services and special prayers and partook of all sacraments without fail. They never uttered a word against God, even though the worst had happened to them. 'The Lord has given and the Lord has taken away; blessed be the name of the Lord,' they would say.

When he saw Annie's eyes wet with tears, as she came out of the church after service, Samuel Sir once again felt how helpless and feeble was humankind.

When Samuel Sir reminded her that she had been crying, Annie, plastering a pale smile on her lips, wiped her tears with the end of her scarf.

'Come, child.' Rosamma placed her hand on Annie's shoulder.

As they descended the hill, silence came with them.

But after a while, Samuel Sir, recovering his cool, said lightly to Annie, 'You will have your exam results in a week, mind you.'

'Annie will pass. What then?' asked Rosamma.

'I will come with the cane if you don't secure a first class. I won't mind that you are a big girl.'

Annie was not that confident. She had written all the subjects fairly well. The rest was...

'Yohannan is not like her. He is living in a dream world. Can't say what is wrong with him. Though not at all lazy, something is wrong. Next year he has to be tackled properly.'

'Maybe because there is no one to watch over him,' said Rosamma.

'It seems he had a close affinity with Paolo*chettan*, who unfortunately—' Samuel Sir stopped abruptly.

'Why recall those things?' said Rosamma, feeling it might hurt Annie.

Meanwhile, Annie became pale. Samuel Sir noticed it and soon changed the subject to avoid embarrassing her.

'Annie, come and have a coffee with us. Go home after that. We have a whole bunch of ripe bananas ready.'

Annie smiled.

'Sir, I will come some other day. There is nobody at home.'

'Then I won't compel you. Let us see if Rosamma and I can finish those fruits on our own.'

'It will be pretty hard,' Rosamma said.

Annie stood for some time, watching the schoolmaster and his wife go, talking and laughing as if they had overcome all their cares. Then she turned homeward.

Yohannan seems to have gone out much earlier than usual. He may be wandering around alone. Only at dusk will he come home. What a boy! I must tell him what Samuel Sir said. Father is not in the least bothered about him. Like Samuel Sir said, Grandfather was his companion. He was brought up by Grandfather. He had been with him from his very infancy. Whenever Father wanted to punish him and would start beating him on account of some mischief, Grandfather would intervene and drive Father away with words like, 'Leave him to me. I will tackle him.' Then he would pick him up, saying, 'Come, you little butt.' Grandfather used to hoist him onto his shoulder, even when he was 10. You felt like giving him a whack on the head when he grinned at you from Grandfather's shoulder.

Since Grandfather's death—how unnatural it was!—Yohannan, feeling lonely, has been simply wandering around most of the time. Still, he regularly attends the church and catechisms.

'Annie, wait, I'm also going your way, we can walk together,' called Mary from her father Lazar*chettan*'s shop, breaking Annie's chain of thoughts.

'You have had coffee at the shop, haven't you?' asked Annie.

'Oh, I simply dropped in,' Mary laughed.

Of late, there has been some change in Mary, thought Annie. Her face and body have a fresh shine and a glow as never before. She seems to have grown physically.

'Hey, next week we have the exam results, Samuel Sir told me.'

'Oh! I know what it will be like.' Mary showed no interest at all. She was so sure of what the result would be.

'Of what use is the result?' Annie said, quite listlessly.

'What! You are sure to pass, even if everyone else in the school fails.'

'That's not it. In my case, it doesn't matter what result I get. I won't be allowed to study further. It is not a question of spending money...for things at home...Father simply won't allow it. But I want to study and I'm willing to go anywhere to do it.'

'Who will take care of the household, once you go away to study?'

'That's what he says. As for me, I have no answer.'

'But can you stay in the family home forever?' Mary asked with a suggestive smile. Annie understood what she meant. She was not eager to marry early.

As they walked and talked, Nina*chen* came straight toward them. Mary's face beamed with joy when she saw him. At the same time, she was a little worried that Annie was with her.

Nina*chen* greeted them with a bright smile. As he approached Mary, his smile became gentler and more enigmatic. Mary's eyelashes fluttered, but Annie did not notice the changing expressions on her face.

'Been to church?' Nina*chen* asked. As he walked away, he nodded to Mary as if suggesting something. Mary stealthily turned to look at Nina*chen*, whose eyes at the same moment turned to lock with hers. In that instant, their eyes spoke volumes.

Samuel Sir had predicted correctly—when the results came, Annie had a first class. The school had a 67 per cent pass. Last year it was 72. Nobody knew what happened. This year, there were only two first classes; last year there were ten.

'The general standard is falling every year,' Sister Mithria said to Sister Marianos, making an evaluation of the results.

'Strict parental supervision is badly needed in childhood,' responded Sister Marianos.

'Most of the children have developed an interest in several other things that distract them from studies,' Sister Mithria pointed out, with supporting examples.

The fact that Molly Sebastian, who came from a relatively distant place, started every day from home at the usual time and instead of coming to school, spent time in the company of two boys in some dense bamboo grove; the illustrated porn magazine seized from Tony Mathew; the love letter that C.T. Kurian wrote to Mary Philip—all these remained closely guarded secrets. Since Sister Marianos knew all these stories, Sister Mithria did not describe them to her in detail. Instead, she only hinted at them.

'Sister, don't you remember Molly Sebastian? And the case of Tony Mathew? The love letter Mary Philip received is still kept in the school office.' Sister Marianos agreed that these were the reasons for the fall in the standard of education.

'Only a few children stand apart,' said Sister Marianos, 'like Annie.'

Thoma growled when he heard that Annie had a first class. Annie stood leaning against the door frame expecting something more. But she was disappointed. He left without saying anything.

Having heard someone calling, Annie came to the veranda and was perplexed to see *Kochachen*, whom she never expected.

'Isn't Thoma*chen* here?'

'He went out somewhere. *Kochachen*, please sit down.'

Before Mathew could say that he was not staying, Annie ran into the kitchen to make coffee. Though he made one or two attempts to leave, he hesitated to embarrass Annie. One must not dishearten a girl, he thought, seating himself on the wooden chair beside the table on the veranda.

'Will Thoma*chen* be late? Then I will meet him later,' he said fairly loudly, and added that she should not trouble about coffee. But there was no answer from the kitchen. He cast his eyes around on the wall, the pillars, and the bamboo curtain. On the wall was a framed photograph of Annie and Yohannan as little children. Annie wore a scarf around her neck and a cheerful smile on her face. But Yohannan was evidently afraid of the camera. Behind them was a painted backdrop with two splendid columns.

Mathew smiled and picked up the notebook lying on the table. Its edges were coloured red with colour pencils.

He thought it was a school notebook, but when he glanced briefly at the first page he was amazed.

As we part and go our separate ways along lonely footpaths, we strive to remember the things we have abandoned and left behind.

Not so easy to separate our souls?

We cannot part our ways?

'*Ayyo*!' Annie cried at the doorstep. She was overcome by shame and fear, as if a secret had been discovered.

'Oh, that! I just—' Annie tried to say something, but she did not know what to say.

'I never knew you could write. It is excellent!'

'*Kochachen* is making fun of me.'

'Not at all, I said it very honestly.' Annie's enquiring glance found not a shadow of scorn on his face. She was relieved, but the flush on her cheeks and the fright in her eyes lingered.

'I also used to write when I was in college. Some stories were published in the weeklies. I got a prize for the best story in a state-level competition. But later, it became different. Sometimes you feel disillusioned.' He disclosed to her his private world without knowing what he was doing. His eyes held a moist shade of tender sorrow. His voice trailed off, overcome by feeling. He sat silently for a while with his head bowed, eyes on his cassock.

'I am also trying to remember the things I have left behind. Annie, do you know—' He simply sat there for a while without completing his words, reflecting on why he should say these things to this girl.

Annie stood dumbfounded, her eyes on his face.

Everything was quite unexpected. Mathew had never intended to reveal his thoughts to anyone. Nor was Annie prepared to listen. Perhaps he would have ended his life without saying anything to anyone. Annie might have carried on in her own way without learning that such disturbing thoughts were vexing the young priest of the parish. Now, quite unexpectedly, all these things became impossible. Gloom descended on their faces. Annie silently went inside and came back with coffee and a few Poovan bananas. She placed them on the table. She thought Mathew's eyes seemed wet. She avoided looking at him directly, to save him from any possible embarrassment or awkwardness. As he sipped his coffee, he recalled his mind to its old track.

'We are planning to start a parallel college here this year. Yesterday, the Vicar and I met some of the local notables, who promised all kinds of support. I have come to meet Thoma*chen* also about this,' he said, not looking at Annie.

'I will tell him when he comes,' she managed to say.

Finishing his coffee, he got up and waited as if he wanted to say something. Then, picking up Annie's notebook, he glanced across its cover.

'You won't mind if I take this with me?' He lifted his face toward Annie. She smiled helplessly. He turned to leave. She stood transfixed until he disappeared among the trees. She could see the branches swaying and the leaves floating in the wind.

The wind blew as if it were bringing a message from someone. Annie held up the mirror and looked eagerly into it. Her face filled the mirror. She found on her face the overflowing feelings of wonder and sorrow her heart had spilt out. She tried desperately to smile.

A two-roomed building, Chullipparampans' house, lay vacant opposite Isaac's pub. A doctor and his family had lived there until last summer. The doctor shut down his clinic and went away, taking his family with him, since the parish had very few patients. After that, a training centre for sewing was started under the supervision of the nuns. That did not succeed either. It was followed by an abortive attempt by an ex-service man, a distant relative of Lazar, who rented the space to open a grocer's shop there. At that time, he received a confidential message from the postman and he simply disappeared. The building lay vacant.

The full responsibility of running the parallel college fell on the shoulders of Mathew, the Assistant Vicar. He did not hesitate to take it up. A postgraduate in English language and literature, he often nursed the thought of becoming a college lecturer. He felt half-relieved when some of the schoolteachers and Jacob Cherian, a raw graduate and job seeker, offered their help. New furniture was made. The veranda was enclosed with blue curtains. Before long, classes began.

Perhaps Annie was the one to whom the college appealed the most. Clad in a half-sari and holding her books close to her chest, she came to classes along with the other girls. As the classes advanced, the boys grew a little grim and the girls became more tender-hearted. Some calf loves sprouted among them. A letter written by a boy called Jose to a girl called Rose Mary never reached its addressee. That was the only notable disaster. And it came to pass that the letter enjoyed some limited private circulation.

'Hey, me too, take me too!' Michael shouted. It was raining. He was standing on the veranda of the parallel college. Seeing Yohannan, he ran to the safety of his umbrella. Michael held Yohannan close to him, his hand around Yohannan's waist.

Yohannan was in a dilemma. He sincerely hated Michael for his rude behaviour. Michael was older than most of the children in the school. He fondled a very thin and neatly cut moustache. He shaved his face twice a week.

Michael began, 'I had a pleasurable time yesterday. In the evening, at it started to rain, I went to abandoned house of the Chullipparampans. Clara had promised to come there. She kept her word and came at dusk. But she was terribly frightened. She wanted to leave immediately and was about to run away, fearing someone might see us. Then I picked her up in my arms and carried her into the house with her feet kicking. She cried silently. I pressed my mouth over her lips and she stopped crying. We spent a lot of time there.'

It seemed to Yohannan that Michael was lying. He was in the habit of spinning yarns and all his cock-and-bull stories were about girls.

'You suppose, all girls are alike, don't you? But they are not. Shhh…Jessy is coming. Walk a little slow. Let's fall behind and follow her.'

Jessy emerged from the footpath on the left and entered the road in front of the boys. Her frock and the back of her jacket were soaking wet. Her legs below the knees were shining in the rain. Sucking his lower lip, Michael made a sound and said, 'If I had her now like this—.'

He held Yohannan tightly and squeezed him closer. Yohannan could stand it no more. He tried to wriggle away. But Michael did not let him go. Running his fingers over Yohannan's cheeks and lips he asked sarcastically, 'You don't know any of these things, do you?'

One day, Yohannan saw a new boy sitting on his left, in class. He was Joshi, son of Daniel and Esther. They had moved here from another parish. They had taught their son from early childhood to fear God and to keep away from all kinds of sin.

Joshi sat near Yohannan and paid close attention to Samuel Sir. When Samuel Sir took a piece of chalk and turned to the blackboard, Michael said something to Yohannan from the back bench. Yohannan kept mum, refusing to turn back.

Daniel had bought some land on the east of the parish. He came to the parish three times to settle the deal and register the sale deed before bringing Esther and the children. They all stayed with a distant relative until their own house was ready.

Daniel and Esther had three children besides Joshi—Agnes, Susan, and Valsamma. All of them praised God in one voice.

Joshi's heart was ever prayerful. His eyes reflected what his heart felt. What appealed to Yohannan most were his eyes. On the very first day during the interval, Yohannan, resting his hand on Joshi's shoulder, showed him the school and the surroundings. He described the teachers and the nuns. He pointed out those who were to be feared. At mid-day, they sat together for lunch.

Joshi's sisters—all had the same look as he had. He introduced them to Yohannan. By evening, he and Yohannan were thick as thieves. Yohannan felt absolutely miserable parting with Joshi in the evening, though they were to meet again the following day. At night, he thought of Joshi. He lay sleepless far into the night. He pictured Joshi's cute and clean face, the oily strands of hair falling on his forehead, and his sparkling, vivid eyes. It poured outside. He knew it in the dark from the sound it made. Darkness drained away from his eyes.

The house and its walls disappeared. Angels flapped their wings around him. One of the angels sounded the trumpet. Another came and gently wiped the tears from his eyes.

Next morning, Yohannan started for school earlier than usual. It was raining heavily, but he kept walking. By the time he reached school, he was soaking wet. Louis, the peon, was opening the doors one by one. After a while, Michael arrived. Standing by the window, he immediately lighted a beedi and puffed out the smoke. 'Yesterday, Clara told me to marry her at the earliest. She locked me in a tight embrace and cried a lot. I believe, it is time to let her off the hook. Another one has taken the bait.'

Yohannan did not look at him. Joshi came late. He was puffing and panting. He must have been running.

'Tomorrow, I must start a bit more early,' Joshi said to himself as he laid his books on his desk. The bell rang. The first period was Samuel Sir's English class. The first thing he did was to ask questions on the previous day's lessons. Severe caning awaited those who failed to give the right answer. All the pupils who attended his class came well prepared, after thoroughly reading the lessons; even Michael. You had to cover your mouth to hide your laughter, when Michael recited poems in a faltering manner, affecting a look of innocence. No, you couldn't laugh; you were more afraid of Michael than of Samuel Sir.

It was Michael who went out with Joshi during the interval. Yohannan became greatly disturbed when he saw Michael walking with his hand on Joshi's shoulder. Would he speak to Joshi about Clara and the like? Afraid of this, and occasionally raising his eyes toward them, Yohannan walked some distance behind them. Michael could have taken another umbrella when going out.

Yohannan later told Joshi that Michael had a bad character, but Joshi himself got a chance to understand that when Michael secretively gave him a book. Its cover had a nude photograph. *Nurse with an Unquenchable Thirst* was the title of the book. Joshi's face turned white with fear as the book was put into his hand.

'Read it later. Put it inside the desk drawer, quick. Don't show it to anyone,' Michael said in a low voice.

But Joshi immediately handed it back and later told Yohannan about it. The way Joshi dealt with Michael filled Yohannan with admiration. Yohannan thought of getting Michael soundly thrashed by complaining to Samuel Sir, but he was afraid at the thought of Michael's revenge. Joshi agreed with him. Yohannan told him that Michael got such dirty books from Barber Lohitakshan. Those books were tucked behind the only mirror in his barbershop, which stood on four stilts, like a treehouse.

'I will never go there for a haircut,' Joshi said in his characteristic slow manner.

Yohannan felt like kissing him on the eyes.

I withheld the rain three months before the harvest. I sent the rain upon one city and withheld it from another. I caused it to rain upon one field; and the field upon which it did not rain was withered away. Two or three cities went to another city to drink water, but were not satisfied. Yet, you have not returned unto me, says the Lord. I have smitten you with blasting and mildew. The palmerworm devoured your gardens and vineyards, and your fig trees and olive trees. Yet, you have not returned unto me, says the Lord…

Yohannan was amazed when he saw this indictment inscribed in Joshi's notebook in a beautiful handwriting. Joshi said that he simply copied it from the book of prophecy.

On that day, Yohannan learned that Joshi and his sisters used to sing in a gospel band, performing on street corners. Yohannan could imagine Joshi standing in the dust and noise of a street, raising a pitch on his instrument, and singing 'I cry from the heart deep' and 'His eyes look after the sparrows' with a full heart. He imagined Joshi heaving sighs and shedding tears as he sang…

Yohannan reached for his hand and held it tight. When he felt Joshi's fingertips, it struck a chord as if the strings of a violin were sonorously waking within. Joshi looked at him and smiled miserably. Yohannan's eyes too were filled with grief. 'Do not take away your song from me,' he prayed silently.

The night throbbed around him. Joshi, wearing green shorts and a shirt printed with green spots, appeared with a slight smile on his petal-like lips. Yohannan took his hand and held it close to his chest. He ran his fingers through Joshi's glistening hair. The fingers wandered down along the nape of his neck and on to his ears. They patted his cheeks and felt the almost invisible down upon his upper lip; they fondled his silken eyebrows and eyelashes and caressed his warm and welcoming lips. Yohannan's balmy breath fell on his cheeks. He felt the body quickening and pressed his lips on the eyes and the mouth, again and again…

And it came to pass that they walked along holding their hands, lacing their fingers, until they reached the riverbank. Undressing and throwing off their clothes, they dipped into the river. The river eyed their bodies sanctified by the grace of God.

They knew each other. As they stood face to face in the neck-deep water seeking each other, the river rose in a flash flood. Overwhelmed by the current, they became separated and started drifting away. Yohannan stretched out his hands and cried, 'Stop, stop!' But Joshi was far ahead. It was dark. There was no other sound, save the fearful rush of the reckless tide. He could see only the darkened glimmer of the river.

He stretched out his hands and searched for Joshi. 'Joshi, Joshi!' he called out. There was no reply. He flowed with the bottomless frenzy of the maddened current. He passed innumerable whirlpools and turnings and reached a vast, desolate sea of sand. He lay fainting with his face buried in the sand.

The Holy Saint has said, if a man has long hair, it is a shame unto him; and if a woman has long hair, it is a glory to her, since it is given to her for a covering. Good. Let me have a haircut, then.

On the way to the barber's shop, Yohannan came across Jessy Abraham. Jessy, who had beautiful, luxuriant hair, studied in Yohannan's class. She could sing and dance fairly well, but she had no self-confidence. She faltered before her teachers. She would begin to cry if they slightly faulted her or looked at her a little disapprovingly. Standing firm against the urgings of Michael, she conducted herself well in the ways of order and sanctity, hoping for a life of inner peace and quiet.

Jessy walked past Yohannan. He looked at her exquisitely elegant body without error or blemish of sin. He did not burn with desire upon her. In her name, sin did not pollute him. He protected himself in sanctity.

When Yohannan reached the barber's shop, Lohitakshan was not there. He must be around somewhere nearby. He is not likely to go very far. Anyway, I'll wait till he returns… Yohannan slowly climbed the steps.

Inside were two stools and an unusually tall wooden chair, facing a wooden ledge fitted across the wall. On this ledge were kept the barber's scissors, stone, powder tins, and so on. On three sides were walls made of planks. At first sight, it looked like a tree house.

He seated himself on the chair and looked at the slanting mirror, tied with a rope to a nail in the wall. In the space between the wall and the mirror, he saw a number of books printed on cheap paper. He took one of them out and turned the pages.

It was the story of a girl who studied in the convent boarding school. Before he could gather complete facts about this girl, postman Peter came there with letters tucked into the plastic cover of an old diary. His umbrella was hooked on his shoulder. Hurriedly, Yohannan tucked the book behind the mirror.

'Isn't Lohitakshan there?' Peter called from outside.

'He's gone somewhere.'

'You didn't see him?'

'No.'

'Oh, then I'll have the shave later.'

Then Lohitakshan emerged from the shrubbery with the weariness of an ejaculation. A pale smile was plastered on his face. His eyes were reddish.

'Where have you been?' asked Peter suspiciously, looking him up and down.

Lohitakshan was unable to give a clear answer.

'Oh, just out.'

'Have you been reading any of those porn books just now?'

'Oh, Peter*chettan* is always joking.'

'You and your tricks... You are corrupting the children with these porn books. Yesterday, I saw one of them by the river—'

'*Chettan*, please come in and sit down.'

'Standing hidden behind a tree, he was peeping at Celinamma, daughter of Muthukattil Pappa*chen*, bathing in the river. I caught him by the ear. You should have seen the fright on his face.' Laughing out loud, Peter climbed the steps.

'Yohannan, can you wait a little?' asked Lohitakshan.

'Yes.' Yohannan got down from the chair.

'Take a stool and wait at the foot of the anjili tree.'

'Give him a book also if he wants.'

Pretending not to hear what they said, Yohannan walked toward the foot of the anjili tree. The wind was blowing. The shade was dense and cool.

He heard Peter say something that made Lohitakshan laugh. Yohannan turned to look. Laughing, Lohitakshan wound a towel around Peter's neck and covered his chest. Peter's face became white with shaving lather. Then Yohannan saw Yakob emerging from the shrubs on the northern side of the road.

A habitual wanderer, Yakob was seen all over the parish. At night, he would lay his head wherever he chose. He had a house among the rocks. He called it 'my nest in a rock'. Since his mother died of illness five years ago, he ceased to have any responsibilities. He owned some farmland. He was quite content with it. But he had the despicable habit of prophesying and crying out about whatever evil happened in the parish. He dreamt of a parish where the barns would be overflowing and the vats would brim over with wine, he said...

The parishioners generally ignored Yakob, who was in the habit of speaking boldly and pointing his scrawny finger at everything. They called him a troublemaker, a cheap advocate, an idealist, and a cynic. Sometimes, he fought with the Vicar. He had on several occasions publicly expressed his dissatisfaction with church governance and the general life of the parish.

In talking about Yakob, Isaac often quoted the proverbs from the Book of Numbers—'Surely there is no witchcraft against Jacob' and 'How can I curse him whom God has not cursed?' Though he quoted inappropriately, he did so only in front of innocent and submissive drunks, so he was never challenged. When somebody once told Yakob about it, he said, 'How can you think that what he says is untrue?'

Peter believed that Yakob's mind became disturbed since he lost Sara. He would occasionally cry out that it was the wickedness of the parish, the diocese and the Holy Church that led the remarkably beautiful Sara to become the wife of the sickly Skaria. But, for lack of evidence, Peter was unable to prove that Yakob desired Sara before her marriage. Yakob had once quite touchingly told Peter that Sara's married life was a glaring instance of incompatibility and a disgrace to the parish.

Peter saw Yakob and said, 'I have been looking for you the last two days. Where were you?'

Yohannan followed Yakob toward the shop. Yakob asked, 'Why were you looking for me so urgently?'

Leaning on the wall, he lighted a beedi. Yohannan paid meticulous attention to his every movement.

Peter's reply was delayed by Lohitakshan's shaving knife, which went into action upon his face. Yakob turned to look.

'I have got a gun. I thought we could go hunting.'

'Don't you get stray cats nowadays?' asked Yakob.

Peter loved cats. Most days, after delivering letters, he came home dangling a cat by its nape. The cat never knew that it was its last journey.

Peter counted eating cats as the secret of his health. His dark stumpy physique, looking like carved black wood, validated that belief of his. His small face was grossly disproportionate to his trunk. He wore a thin, neatly cut moustache on the thick skin above his upper lip. The rest of his face was almost empty. His cheeks were always twitching. And they said he was given to whoring.

'So, what have you decided?'

'Agreed.'

'What if we are lucky enough to get a tusker or a boar?'

Peter was not as good a marksman as Yakob. Besides, he had a general distrust of the night. Presumably he went about whoring at daytime, while on duty.

'Can we go tonight?'

'No, I have to go elsewhere.'

'Then tomorrow.'

'Done.'

Sara came like a vision. The stones on the path and the trees on the wayside knew she was coming. Covering her head with the end of her sari, Sara walked with slow steps. She had a packet of medicines in her hand. Her husband Skaria had been bedridden for a long time. She was exceedingly God-fearing. Nothing ever shook her faith.

'Look at Sara,' said Yakob.

Yohannan looked. He was far from sure that it was to him that Yakob spoke. After the shave, Peter looked in the mirror and powdered his face. Standing behind him, Lohitakshan watched Peter. Both of them heard Yakob's commandment.

Sara came like a vision.

Taking a few steps forward, Yakob called, 'Sara!'

Quite taken aback by someone on the roadside calling her, Sara turned and saw him. Yakob! God-fearing Sara was startled and turned her face away. Yakob flinched. Disillusioned by Sara's rebuff, he returned to the support of the wall. He sat on the ground, drained and shattered. His face darkened.

'Sara is in danger. Almost everyone in the parish is against her. Who is there who will pray for her?' Yakob mumbled to himself. 'Her womb will never be blessed...'

Yakob's words filled Yohannan with fear. That Sara was in some grave danger; that all ought to have sympathized with her; that there were no blessings on her—he stood there anxiously.

'That packet in her hands is medicine for Skaria. He is lying there on the coir bed, moaning and groaning. Perhaps, Philipos's mother is watching over him.'

Yakob's voice was tinged with anguish, anger and shame. The circles of his eyes waxed and waned to the tune of his words. His chin trembled. The veins on his arms became taut. Frightened, Yohannan looked into the barber's shop.

Peter and Lohitakshan were not listening to Yakob. Yes, they did hear his first commandment, 'Look at Sara.' But, as she passed, they returned to their former positions. Peter continued to powder his face. Lohitakshan patted the back of Peter's shirt and neck with a towel under the pretext of removing hairs.

Gradually, Yakob's voice resounded in Yohannan's ears like the voice of a prophet.

'Skaria does not deserve compassion. He lived in wickedness. Illness, it is true, is a punishment for his sins. But did poor Sara do anything wrong? Did she do any evil?'

After a pause he continued. 'Sara is the exemplary woman in the parish. No other woman in this parish has her beauty. No young girl has her endearing charm. Why does God make her suffer?'

Then, Yakob went his way.

Yohannan stood looking at the remains of the burnt candles in front of the big stone cross erected on the roadside. The cross was as tall as him. He imagined a dove perching on its top with a green leaf in its beak, plucked from green groves.

It must be an olive leaf from a tree in a grove in some valley far away.

Yohannan wondered why an olive branch came to his mind. He thought about it for a long time. I have never seen an olive leaf in my life. There is no possibility of seeing one ever. There may be valleys somewhere on earth where olive trees grow. But I will never go there. Still my mind dreams of an olive leaf. And that in the middle of this commotion.

The din and bustle of the feast was all around him. People strolled among the bamboo and thatch stalls decorated with cycad leaves dancing in the wind. The place echoed with festive sounds. The souls of the dead came out from their tombs and sat in the sun. The souls of the poor dead struggled through the earth and came out of their graves. They sat throbbing over their graves, where they had been lying asleep for a long time. They looked at the earth and sky and wept. They stretched their earth-stained fingers toward those who passed them along the decorated paths. A pale mist spread over the cemetery. But no one saw it.

No one saw Yohannan either, except Joshi.

Yohannan saw several familiar faces pass him by along the path. No one seemed to notice him. Nobody called him or put their hands on his shoulder. He felt pity for himself and wept in his heart. Then, quite unexpectedly, he felt a thin hand upon his shoulder—long, lean, ruddy fingers.

Joshi!

Joshi was standing behind him with a smile sparkling like rain drops. Yohannan held back a cry that nearly escaped his lips. While I was wandering aimlessly alone, a loving bird has descended upon my shoulder. A bird…

'This is Yohannan.' Joshi introduced him to his father and mother.

It was then that Yohannan saw them. Behind them were Agnes, Susan, and Valsamma. They stood like light in darkness.

'Not a day passes without his mentioning you, son. Why don't you come and visit us? Do come one day,' Esther said. Yohannan felt something fluttering up from deep in his heart.

'I will,' he said.

'Who else lives with you?'

'Father and sister.'

A wind from the cemetery blew toward them, a wind icy and shivering like a sob.

'Mother is dead and gone.'

'Oh!' Esther sorrowed. Moving close to Yohannan, she ran her fingers through his hair. Yohannan became a babe for whom smiling, crying, and silence were the only language. He looked toward Joshi, who stood there wearing his characteristic smile upon his lips.

'You two carry on. We will go a different way. Shall we?' asked Daniel.

Joshi nodded his head.

Linking arms, Yohannan and Joshi set off across the open fields spread before them, bathed in the cool shade of friendship. They went past the old woman selling bread, remembering the sweetness that her cookies left melting on their tongue. Swept by the wind of prayerfulness they knelt at the altar, which was throbbing with light; they felt grains of sand biting their knees.

Quite accidently, seeing Sara kneeling in prayer a little to his left, Yohannan tried to recall something he had forgotten. He remembered a thick hardbound book on art the Vicar had once allowed him to skim through. It was full of prints of old masters. The sight of Sara kneeling by the altar reminded him powerfully of one of the pictures in that book.

He stood still on the road, watching Joshi walk home with his parents and sisters. Loneliness took root and grew into a thickly-leaved plant once again in his mind. He turned to see Sara coming slowly down the path, her head covered with the end of her sari.

Sometimes, I wish I could speak to the leaves, the stones, and the water. I can talk to them quite undisturbed however long I want to. But that does not suffice. Should I not try to understand what they have to tell me? Who knows how this leaf trembling in silence, this stone lying in the grass, and this flowing water passed the night?

The river calls up something lying dormant in the heart. When I look at the river through the gaps in the leaves, I feel someone's fingers reaching out to touch my heart. My eyes tremble.

Cool water surrounds me. I feel the whole world shrinking into me.

If anyone asks you, 'What are you doing?' give him the reply, 'Don't disturb me. I am out here knowing myself.'

I crave for a sudden rain from the sky. I will sit here soaking wet in the rain. I will not seek even the cover of a leaf. I will sit upon these stones uncovered, unclothed.

A grazing little lamb among the nearby thickets stood looking at me. Its eyes were filled with wonder. It asked me, 'What are you doing?' I took on the question with a tired smile, 'Don't disturb me. I am out here knowing myself.'

There was endless silence all around. Not a word was uttered to break it. When I beckoned the lamb with my hand it turned and ran away. The wind moved among the clouds.

Yohannan heard Mary calling him. He did not see the buffaloes hidden behind the thickets. Mary too might be sitting under some dark shadow. Perhaps she was crying.

He stood firmly on the grass wondering why she called him. He looked suspiciously at Mary, who chewed a leaf as she came toward him.

Her eyes were troubled. Unoiled strands of hair strayed on to her forehead. Her sweat glistened in the sun. He dropped his eyes when she looked straight at him.

'Haven't you heard?'

'What?' he asked her.

'Nina*chen* is getting married.'

'Yes, I heard.'

Yohannan had heard that Nina*chen* was engaged to a girl called Philomena. When he heard it he had in fact thought of Mary.

'What of that?'

She understood what he was driving at. She smiled sadly.

'People are of different kinds. Still I thought…' she said to herself. 'I can die if I want. There are stories galore of such deaths too. But I cannot die… Not that I am afraid… I cannot…'

Yohannan stood stupefied. Mary stripped herself of all clothing.

'He thinks he has deceived a girl. Dirty pig…' Unable to control herself she swore and cursed Nina*chen* with anger and sorrow.

Yohannan was stunned. He saw her body. It was uncovered and naked. His eyes winked.

'Kiss me on my forehead,' she said.

He did not move.

'Kiss me on my breasts,' she said.

He still stood bewildered.

'Lie down with me.'

She knelt on the ground.

'Can you sin to God?'

He raised his head and looked up at the heavens. Then she left him and ran away. 'I have dreamed a dream. There is no one to interpret it to me,' he said to himself.

Annie sat in her room reading. Hearing soft footsteps behind her, she turned and saw Yohannan. He was about to leave the room stealthily, without drawing her attention.

'Where have you been?' Annie asked him.

He thought of what to tell her.

'Simply wandering about, aren't you? You are not at all learning your lessons. Can't you sit here and read them?'

He simply stood there pressing his fingers against the wall.

'Omana told me you are very poor in mathematics.'

He stared at Annie.

'Sit here. I will give you a sum.'

'No, I can't.'

After that Annie had nothing to say. She wiped her face with her hands and came out of the room, putting her half-sari neatly in place. Yohannan followed her to the veranda.

'Look how father walks.' Annie put her hand on a pillar and looked toward the road.

Thoma walked with faltering steps. When he stopped in the courtyard, he was unable to stand firm on the ground. Unwinding the cotton towel from his head, he wiped the sweat from his face.

'Why are you standing like this, Annie?' He stepped on to the veranda and sat on the coir bed. Unable to face his daughter, he sat with his head bowed, utterly filled with self-contempt.

'Fetch me some water. I feel dry.'

When Annie went in to fetch water, Yohannan stepped out into the courtyard, unable to stand alone in front of his father.

He ran his fingers over the planks of the empty pigsty.

The sow and her piglets may be wandering around, Yohannan thought. Do I hear them cry?

As he pricked his ears up, he heard his father's slurred words. 'I know, instead of giving love to my dear ones, I have only repelled them, knowingly or unknowingly. After all, is there anything lovable about this Thoma, an unclean, headstrong scoundrel? When Theresa was alive, I woke up on many nights to see her crying, clasping my feet. Once, losing patience, I kicked her on the face. I remember it. I kicked her. Yet, she never grumbled or abused me. I hurt her a lot. May her soul rest in peace! I think she might have forgiven me. Her heart was so pure. It was all torn and racked with pain by the time of her death, I know, I know.'

'Father, what are you babbling? You are drunk today, aren't you?' Annie grumbled.

He looked at his daughter wearily. Once again he returned to himself. 'These are no babblings of a drunk. I am having a session with myself, a confession where I am both the speaker and the hearer.'

'I don't understand any of these things.'

'Neither do I.'

Yohannan walked leisurely, as he was in no hurry. Then he came upon Nina*chen* leaving the church after his marriage to Philomena, the daughter of Pathrose. A group of parishioners walked with him. Yohannan stopped to look at the procession. Philomena the bride, dressed in white, walked under an umbrella someone held over her. The others were laughing and talking.

A smile of joy and a feeling of satisfaction shone on Nina*chen*'s lips. He kept glancing covertly at his bride. When Philomena felt his eyes on her, she flinched a little. She became restless. Unable to seek a hiding place elsewhere, she shrank into herself. Perhaps only Yohannan noticed it.

The wedding procession passed him. Yohannan felt he was standing alone in the middle of ruins scattered on a vast plain of sand blown over by a tempest of brimstone and fire.

His mind became listless. A tempest has passed over the plain devastating everything. The fallen stones of the steeples and towers lay scattered all around. I walk along touching every stone within reach. I hear the sighs heaving from the midst of the broken bricks. I see that a city has been completely burnt out. Stones and ashes alone remain. Whose will is this, God's or Satan's?

'Why is this boy so lost in thought?' asked Peter, the postman, who was passing by.

Yohannan evaded the question. By the time he resumed walking he had forgotten everything he had been thinking about till then.

When they looked at him from a distance, they did not recognize him, and they wept aloud. They tore their mantles and threw dust upon their heads. They saw that his suffering was very great and no one spoke a word.

The children became totally unnerved when they heard it at school in the morning. They hesitated to believe it. At first, they laughed it off as a lie and scorned those who broke the news. Each one consoled oneself saying, 'No, it is not likely to be true' and 'It is not possible.' But when the shadow of apprehension darkened their minds, they desperately prayed, 'Lord, may it turn out to be untrue' and 'May that never happen.'

But it was true. The children were convinced from the fallen faces, the deathly silence, and the heaving sobs of the teachers and the nuns.

Then, leaving their classes, the children began to move along in groups. Those who looked from faraway hilltops saw the groups of schoolchildren moving along the footpaths below. They did not know why. They thought that the school might have declared a holiday. But when they noticed that the children were going in the same direction, they were filled with apprehension.

The children marched in silence. No one had anything to say. Even the girls who used to look cheerful and laughing walked without a word.

Yohannan looked at Joshi, who was on the verge of tears. His cheeks were flushed and sweating, and his eyes were wet. Unable to endure it, Yohannan looked away.

Walking past the rubber trees, climbing the stone walls of terraces, and turning to the left, the children came to the courtyard sanctified with lemon trees and plants and flowers. They were exhausted in body and spirit. The girls could not hold back their tears. Those who went into the room came out into the courtyard, crying and pale.

Samuel Sir lay in his room, paralyzed and still. Rosamma, sitting on the floor, buried her face in the bed and wept sore. Some women stood huddled in a corner and cried silently.

Everything crumbled overnight. When the night withdrew her dark embrace, Samuel Sir found himself lying in bed. He did not move when Rosamma came in with the morning black coffee. She left it there, telling him to drink it when he pleased. The coffee had turned cold when she returned to the room after some time. Samuel Sir still lay there. 'What! Are you still in bed?' she asked, approaching him with some mischief in mind. She was frightened to death when she looked at his face. He was struggling to move and say something. Pain blazed on his face. Now and then his eyelids flew open. Tears spilled over the corners of his eyes and fell on the pillow. She stared at him for a while and moved a step toward him as if to ask him something. She was frozen with fright and stepped backwards to the door. She felt as if she were waking from an awful nightmare. Then she ran toward him with a loud cry. She threw herself upon his body. Holding him tightly, she pressed her parched lips on his face and chest. Then tears welled up and blurred his vision.

Unable to stand it, the children retreated with shuddering sobs. Joshi was in tears and was about to turn, his hand on Yohannan's shoulder, when the Vicar, the Assistant Vicar, and other men entered the room. The Vicar approached Samuel and asked, 'What is wrong?'

'What have we done to suffer so cruel a punishment?' Rosamma cried to the Vicar. 'I…I have no one to lean on. First my child…and now…'

'Don't cry. There is nothing to get so anxious about.'

'Don't you see this, Father? He lies dumb and still. Look at his eyes.'

'Rosamma, don't worry. Something might have happened in the night. We will make immediate arrangements to take him to the doctor,' the Vicar said calmly.

'Please do it.'

'Let us pray. The Lord will not abandon us.'

Joshi and Yohannan, standing close to the wall outside, heard the cries and comforting words from within. When the nuns came, the boys made way for them.

Outside, it was sad and gloomy. A pale sun lingered on the hills. No breeze blew and no leaves rustled. People stood in groups in the courtyard or under the trees, speaking in stifled voices. The house stood sore in sorrow, its walls soaked in grief.

Yohannan bent his face. An army of ants marched, carrying a dead insect over a dead leaf.

Yohannan lowered his voice and said, 'Let us walk.'

'Yes.'

Little stones ground under their feet and slid away. They moved steadily like two light shadows until they reached the shade of a tree. Yohannan stopped as if something suddenly occurred to him. He stood silent for a while, scratching something on the bark of the tree. Then he said, lifting his face toward Joshi, 'Whose will is this?'

He gripped Joshi's shoulders.

'Tell me.'

Joshi stared back at him. 'It is God's will.'

Yohannan slapped Joshi, who faltered and fell. He propped himself upon his hands, rose to his feet, and looked at Yohannan with indifference rather than pain.

'Dare say it again.'

'Surely, it is the will of God.'

Yohannan delivered another stinging slap on the other cheek of Joshi, who faltered again and fell. Then Yohannan hurried away.

That same day, Samuel Sir was taken to the hospital in the town. Two weeks later, he was taken elsewhere, we learned. Some of the parishioners visited him occasionally to find out how he was doing. They invariably returned disheartened with no good news.

From the very beginning, the doctors did not entertain the slightest hope. They assured Rosamma that they would do everything medicine could do, but the oldest of them, the orthopaedic, added that everything happens according to the will of God.

When he was released from the hospital, Samuel Sir was not much better. The doctors said that with proper medical care and by the grace of God he might perhaps recover some time in the future.

Just before Samuel Sir was discharged, Mathew, the Assistant Vicar visited the hospital with money. The next day,

Samuel Sir was brought home and the parishioners visited him in the evening. He lay there on the coir bed, babbling and looking at Annie, Yohannan, and others. His eyes filled with tears when he realized he would never be able to walk or speak. Rosamma, eyes clouded in grief, saw this and went near him with a sob. She wiped the tears from his eyes with the end of her sari. Looking into her eyes, he tried to smile.

Somewhere in the woods a voice cried, 'Oh, I wish my grief were weighed, and all my calamity laid in the balances together!'

Yohannan thought, can grief be weighed? Can it be gathered and placed in the balances?

Sobbing, Annie passed him. He stood close to the trunk of a tree. He saw the Vicar, his assistant, and Ephraim walking away silently.

Peter and Yakob passed him with their heads bent. Philipos and Thoma followed. But no one noticed Yohannan.

Night fell. Empty months are allotted to me; and nights of misery are apportioned to me. Agonizing pain that eats into the limbs and is the firstborn of death... thought Yohannan.

Slowly and calmly Joshi walked toward Yohannan. Joshi's eyes were bleary and bloodshot from crying. Letting out a cry like a flowing stream, Yohannan reached out and hugged Joshi to him. They became each other's arms.

'Open to me, my love, my dove, my perfect one...'

She was asleep, but her heart was awake. She arose.

She unbolted the door, but did not see her beloved. 'Where are you?' she called. He gave no answer.

He was gone. 'I will seek him everywhere,' she vowed to herself.

She went out. Her feet, bathed clean before she went to bed, became soiled with dirt. She sought him in the streets and in the squares, but did not find him. Making their rounds in the city, the watchmen found her. They beat her and wounded her. The watchmen of the walls took away her mantle. Still she asked of them which way her beloved had turned. She found him following the footprints of his flock.

In a turning of a steep slope, she found him asleep. He was uncovered. In his right hand was a fruit of lemon.

She stood gazing at him. My beloved, you are beautiful, ah, you are beautiful. But, sapped by some embarrassing thought, she suddenly slumped down and kneeled on the ground.

Then someone called her from outside; at first softly, then fairly loudly. She woke up from her afternoon nap. Thinking it a mere dream, she continued to lie there quietly for a while. Her face was damp with sweat. Stray hairs stuck to her face.

Pricking her ears up, she tried to listen. She heard the bleating of lambs from somewhere. Then there was silence.

'Annie—'

She scrambled to her feet. Oh, Lord! She reset her sari properly and looked into the mirror. She was dismayed to see her face heavy with sleep.

'Annie—'

It was Mathew at the door. Lowering the mirror, Annie stood stupefied.

'Were you sleeping?'

Annie stood bathed in sweat. Her mind was filled with the smell of a flock of sheep.

'Look.'

Mathew held out the lemon in his right hand toward her. Seeing this, she ran a few steps forward and slumped down on her knees.

'No, thanks,' she said. Her eyes filled with tears.

'Annie!' Mathew knelt by her side.

Muffling a cry with her hands, she looked at Mathew.

'Asking me not to love you, aren't you?' Mathew asked her taking her arms in his.

'God will send his curse upon us.' She averted her face, crying.

'What have we done to sin? Girl, don't you know that God is not a man to mistake love for sin?' He cupped her face in his hands and kissed her on the forehead. She touched his shirt. It smelled of frankincense.

When the men of Sodom surrounded his house, Lot had two daughters who had never known a man. A woman who has never known a man is called a virgin.

'Mary!'

'I too had my days of virginity.'

'O Jesus!'

'A fellow has now turned up with a proposal.'

'Who is that?'

'He is a widower, 50-odd years old. Never mind the second marriage. He has money to burn and has three children. Their mother died in her fourth childbirth. So far so good! If she hadn't died, there would have been no such proposal.'

'Get lost and don't make me laugh, will you?'

'Not everyone has the gift of laughter. My parents and neighbours are all furious with me for accepting the proposal. But I told them categorically that it was all I needed.'

'Are you bluffing?'

'No. I am quite serious.'

'I don't understand.'

'You won't understand.'

'Mary!'

'Yes?'

'Have you consented to the marriage proposal?'

'I told you, didn't I?'

'What about your family?'

'Somebody who came to the house mentioned it just for fun. All at once, I said I was willing. They were appalled. When they objected, I threatened to commit suicide. Now it looks like they've almost agreed. It will be a simple wedding. Then I will go away to his house. O, I didn't tell you his name, did I? His name is Raphael, a good name. The eldest daughter has recently been married off. Next is a son 17 years old. The youngest is also a son, but he is mentally challenged. He has never been to school. His father carries him on his shoulders to church every Sunday. Poor fellow!

'What poor fellow! He may be older than your father.'

'So? He has a son who is 17 years old.'

'What do you mean?'

'I can lie with the son whenever the old man's away.'

'O Lord!'

'I will have fun.'

'Are you mad, girl?'

'I don't know, whatever.'

'You're babbling!'

'Why, what did I say?'

'Mary...'

'You cannot trust anything. You cannot trust anyone—not even God.'

'Stop.'

'I'm in a hurry. The buffaloes are there. And I need to bathe too.'

Yohannan overheard everything that went on between them. He stood outside, close to the wall, listening keenly. He looked as if he had taken root there. He saw Mary coming out of Annie's room looking troubled. Warily he looked at her. She bent her face as she left. Yohannan slipped away into his room lest she should see him.

Walking a few steps, Mary turned to look and saw Annie standing at the door like an idol. The house looked like a cage housing an idol. Mary walked away steady and dry-eyed. Stricken with grief, Annie turned toward the kitchen. Then Yohannan slipped out of his room quiet as a shadow.

Yohannan stepped into a faded evening. The sky looked unusually pale. The trees were all dark brown. The leaves were black and yellow. The pigs stood quietly under the trees. Holding their perfectly tuned snouts, they snuffed out every sad or tragic bit of news. Yohannan walked past them. Then he saw an immaculate white bridal dress hanging from a tree. But there was no bride in it. Dangling from a branch, the dress danced slowly in the light wind. Yohannan stood uncertain beneath the dancing veil. All of a sudden, he heard the hilarious laughter of a woman. He looked around, but did not see anyone. He walked along the unpaved road. On either side were withered bamboo groves. Then he saw at a distance a lean and lanky man coming straight toward him. He carried a boy who sat with his legs around the man's neck. Yohannan waited for them to pass. Approaching him slowly, the man said, 'Since it is Sunday, we are going to church.' Sitting on his perch up there, the boy displayed a gaping smile. He made no sound at all. 'I don't know if it is late,' the man said and hurried on. Yohannan stood watching him for some time. Then he turned and went his way. The road ended among the trees on the riverside. He pricked up his ears and heard voices from the river. He looked in the direction of the voices and saw Mary. With her was a lanky boy. They were standing in the water. She was laughing and splashing water toward him. He was panting and stood with his back toward her. For a while she was silent. When he turned, she started laughing and splashing again. He tried to run toward the bank when she held him tightly from behind, pressing her wet breasts upon his back. She undressed him and threw his clothes to the bank. The wet clothes went flying and fell at Yohannan's feet. Looking once again at the river, he turned and walked away. He heard the laughter from the river a fair distance away. Then the sound grew more and more distant and died away. Silence fell around him.

When Yohannan reached home, Annie was nowhere outside. He saw the pigs waiting outside their sty. He opened the door and herded them in. And it came to pass that, lying on the veranda coir bed and beneath the pair of old leather slippers, he wished for darkness to come. And darkness came before long.

Dragging his feet, Thoma trudged along, leaning on Yakob's shoulder. When he faltered, Yakob prevented him from falling. The pigs all grunted when they scented him. 'Why do my pigs grunt?' asked Thoma.

'Are you paying any attention to them nowadays?'

'You told me that...'

'If you neglect them like this...'

'Yes?'

'The pigs will either die or run away.'

'Yes?'

'The sty will become empty.'

'Oh, never mind.'

Then Annie came out with a lighted candle. When Thoma wavered and was about to fall, Yakob held him. Rubbing sleep from his eyes, Yohannan got up from the coir bed. Thoma lay down on it, unmindful of anything. Seeing Annie looking reproachfully at him, Yakob said, 'Daughter, I was not drinking with him, it was someone else. And I don't know if he has a drinking buddy at all.' Looking alternately at Annie and Yohannan, he added, 'He has already suffered unbearable sorrow. More agonizing things are in store for him. He will try to raise himself up. But the more he tries, the more utterly he will fall. Wait and see.' His grim prophecy echoed after he left.

Night separated people from people and things from things. Annie was separated from Yohannan, and Yohannan from Annie. Thoma was alone in another world. Everything disappeared: the walls, the furniture, and the roof of the house. Annie lay with her face buried in the bed, forgetting that it was her bed. Its smell of oil and sweat did not seem familiar to her. As if by some witchcraft, night lulled the frightened girl to sleep. Thoma had gone to sleep early in the night. An intruding candle occasionally disturbed his sleep. Growling in displeasure and shaking his entire body, he would go back to sleep. Lying with his eyes open in the dark, Yohannan began to comfort his body.

The winter is past; the rain is over and gone. The flowers appear on the earth. The time of pruning the vine has come. The voice of the turtledove is heard in our land.

Mathew walked along remembering King Solomon and thinking how sanctified was the evening. The valley was deserted. Lingering here and there were a few spirits. They scrutinized Mathew. One of them observed to a nearby spirit that there was a highly controversial article on Catholic priests in the English newspaper in Mathew's hand.

'Oho!'

'Yes, *Kochachen* is discussing it with the Vicar today.'

'Oho.'

'Yes, but before that...'

When Mathew raised his head, he saw Sister Mithria and Sister Marianos on the slope. For a little while, he lost sight of them among the trees. Then he saw Sister Marianos running after Sister Mithria. 'They are trying to forget something,' Mathew said to himself.

Tucking up her white cloak with her hands, Sister Mithria ran as fast as she could. But Sister Marianos easily outran her and tagged her. Then Marianos turned and ran. After touching Mithria, she turned around and ran. Mithria could not keep pace with her. Marianos hid behind a turning in the path. Sister Mithria wandered among the trees to look for her.

'Look!'

'Yes.'

The spirits silently smiled. Looking up at the slope, Mathew slowly walked along.

Sister Mithria lay on her back under a tree, her hands folded on the cross upon her chest. She lay very still with her eyes shut, feigning death. Gathering green leaves in her cupped hands, Marianos came and stood before Mithria. Then she dropped them ritually on Mithria's face. Green for resurrection, Mathew thought. Mithria could not help but wake up. Hiding a hearty smile within and beating time on his left palm with the folded newspaper in his right hand, Mathew went along the road where the evening sun and the wind were lavish.

'Going away?'

'Yes.'

But an unfortunate thing happened on the way. The spirits had a forewarning of it. Though they knew everything in advance, instead of paying attention to the impending event, they fluttered their tiny wings and followed Mathew.

All of a sudden, an extremely frightened Sara turned a corner and came into Mathew's view. Before he could ask her what happened, he saw Yakob following behind her. Dropping her face, Sara walked on when Mathew called her, 'Sara, tell me, what happened?'

She heard him and stopped, but just a moment. Then she quickened her pace and walked away without turning back. Mathew stood perplexed. Then Yakob spoke from behind.

'I will tell you. Let Sara go.'

Mathew turned to him and spoke sternly. 'Yakob, you shut up. I have understood everything, no matter what you are going to say. You have harassed that woman regardless of her being the wife of another man.'

'I only told her that I love her. I haven't harassed her as *Kochachen* says. Harassing women is not my way.'

'Yakob, don't you know she is the wife of Skaria?'

'Yes.'

'Then what does it mean that you still desire her?'

'I love her, no matter what it means.'

'Isn't it against the commandments of God?'

'How does it violate the commandments of God? How can you say what I have done is wrong? Abandoning so beautiful a woman as Sara in marriage to a good-for-nothing person like Skaria is, in my opinion, the violation. It can be rectified only with the love of another man.'

'What if Sara does not desire it?'

'*Kochachen*, don't take offence at what I say. I'm a little drunk. But don't mind it. You asked me if I would love Sara regardless of her will. My answer is, Sara too has hopes and desires that she represses. Skaria coughs and croaks like an old man. Peter says he is a consumptive, and he may be right. Her life with Skaria is a feat of endurance. Yes, I say Sara is putting up with Skaria. *Kochachen* may ask me why she finds it bearable. She bears it out of fear of the cassocks you and the Vicar wear. Frightened by those priestly robes, she endures that abomination. *Kochachen*, please don't misunderstand me. But I think I must tell you these things. She represses her cravings, afraid of the finger you always point at the congregation when standing in the altar, enrobed in your splendid vestments, in the midst of lighted candles, frankincense fumes, the Holy Book, and the consecrated bread and wine of the Eucharist. She is fearful of your large notions of sin and goodness, vice and virtue. What is a woman going to gain when she is called to eternal rest after wasting away her life with a good-for-nothing fellow? Ha, ha! By the way, I am reminded of a cartoon I have seen somewhere. It is a good cartoon. When I say good, I mean I like it. I am far from sure that others will have the same opinion. I will tell you quickly what it is. Ha, ha! I can't stop laughing when I recollect it. Wait, I'm going to tell you. Two priests are sitting in the abode of God, on a huge cloud high above the earth. They are dressed in their ceremonial robes. One of them sits with his hands clasped on his chest. The other one sits with his left leg resting on the cloud, his left arm on his lap. I remember every detail. Both of them have wings, like the angels have. Around their heads are haloes. At a distance, on either side, are two more clouds, each with a pair of enrobed, winged priests with haloes around their heads. *Kochachen*, do you think these priests are happy they have such a quiet resting place after death and are grateful to God for this? You are wrong if you think so. Do you know what is in their hearts? Depression and emptiness. One of them complains to the other: 'Was it for this that I abandoned a life of wine, women, and music?' If this is what the priests who have earned a heavenly life say, then what will be the lot of a woman like Sara? Of course, I admit it is a mere cartoon, but doesn't it contain a shocking truth? Sara will writhe and cry in heaven. I hope I won't hear it in hell. But you as a priest will have to hear it, because you, fitted with a pair of wings, will be there on a nearby cloud. Ha, ha!'

Yakob burst into cruel laughter. Then he said, 'A world of love is what I hope for: a world free from choked-back tears, stifled thoughts, and smothered truths; a world without impotence and barrenness. A world full of love is what I want.'

Yakob and his words struck Mathew like a revelation. Yakob seemed to blaze from behind the burning bush.

'*Kochachen*, are you going?' Mathew heard Yakob asking. The heavy irony and scorn in his voice was quite obvious. He takes great pride in his own words as truthful and righteous. If he were covered by the deep! If he were overwhelmed by a flood of waters! If he were entombed by the pit!

Mathew felt he had entered a world of fantasy. Was everything a fantasy? Didn't those things really happen? Did not Yakob harass Sara as she went along the road? Didn't she approach me helplessly? Didn't I try to admonish him? And didn't he raise some serious questions to challenge me? Were all those things a mere fantasy? Perhaps they were a figment of my imagination. I might have posed those questions to myself in absolute privacy. Those questions might have had their roots in my own doubts and anxieties. Mathew began to soothe himself in this manner. But the next moment he felt that this kind of self-interrogation was not at all desirable. We must surrender ourselves. It is the commandment. It is the covenant. Mathew felt nearly choked within his cassock. He recalled the story of a mad man, who, holding up a yellow straw, claimed that it was a ray of the sun he had finally secured. He was giving a new meaning to the piece of straw. For him, that meaning was total and decided. He would not concede that it was a straw. It was with a self-defined freedom that he made such a claim. It wasn't so much the existence of the sun's ray that he declared, but his freedom. Hasn't Yakob performed a similar manoeuvre?

The image of Yakob wrapped in a yellow shawl came into Mathew's mind like an awful nightmare. Then, quite accidently, he recalled that Sara also wore a sari with large patches of yellow on it. Yellow was suggestive of sin. It was symbolically entangled with vices, like deceit, jealousy, adultery, and temptation.

Walking along the deserted road, Mathew let his eyes roam from side to side and to the faraway hills. When his eyes rested on the deep, dark greenery, all the gloom and unease fled from his heart. The green force that ran through woods unstirred by the wind, the groves, and the slopes of unbroken green bore witness to the resurrection of the spirit and the grandeur of life. Mathew's face lit up with this regenerating thought. A little while ago, he had looked weary. Mathew climbed the hill with a cheerful face, harbouring an intimate thought in his mind.

'Ephraim, I think I have a temperature. It is getting very cold too.'

Hardly had the Vicar said this, when Ephraim brought out an old sweater and a muffler. The Vicar took the muffler and said he did not want the sweater.

'Father, it is not good to sit by the window in the cold wind. It will cause chest pain.'

The Vicar did not want to move the cane chair away from the window.

'O, never mind. Ephraim may go.'

Ephraim, disapproving, finally obeyed him.

'I will make some coffee with black pepper in it. It is good for a cold.' Ephraim hurried to the kitchen.

The Vicar lay back in his chair, closed his eyes, and drifted into sleep. In his sleep, he began to see things. At first, it was not clear what he saw. There was fog. He looked intently and realized there was a child, a boy. The cold wind continued to blow. Within the wooden walls of the house, the child lay frightened as if he were drowning. Ho, what terrible cold! His teeth chattered. Then he felt a warm hand caressing his chest. He heard his mother crying a mournful prayer, like a never-ending lament. Her tears fell on his forehead and her trembling lips kissed him. The hills are clothed in mist. The trees stand frozen. What pain do the birds feel in their nests on the branches? Are the birds crying?

'Father, are you asleep?' The Vicar opened his eyes. There was wetness on one cheek, which he wiped with his hand. Then he held his hand out toward Ephraim for the coffee.

'Father, your hand is shivering. If you feel too cold, I will go to the valley and...'

'No, don't be bothered about me.' After taking a sip of the coffee, he leaned back on the chair again. 'It was the same in my childhood. Now I am old. Hey, this coffee is good. Did you have some?'

'There is some more here. I'll bring you more if you want. Or I will keep it in the flask, so that you can have it at night.'

When he was about to shut the door, Ephraim saw *Kochachen* coming up the hill.

Outside, the wind blowing past the green pastures whispered something to the earth. The birds flew to their mountains. The clouds passed the information to other clouds. Silence filled the hills, like a hymn without words.

The Vicar sat with a troubled mind. Mathew took a seat in front of him. In his hand also was a cup of Ephraim's herbal coffee. The Vicar guessed that his assistant wanted to discuss something with him. Sipping his coffee, Mathew held the newspaper toward his senior.

'Father, go through the article in this paper. In fact, it has raised some serious doubts in my mind.'

With a light smile, the Vicar took the paper from Mathew's hand. The specific article filled a whole page of the weekend magazine. There were two illustrations with churches in the background.

The article began with the problems in a parish. A 30-year-old priest, despite warnings, persisted in having an intimate relationship with a woman. When he was called to the bishop's house for the ultimate procedure of disciplinary action, he defrocked himself and left, leaving his cassock behind. Later, he married the woman. The writer of the article analyzed the consequences of this incident. He made an impressive list of difficulties that priests had to face when they decided to end their celibacy and get married. The author presented arguments for and against celibacy, collecting opinions from several priests in active service. This is what the Vicar gathered from a cursory glance through the page. Then, with a faint smile, he raised his face toward Mathew, who winced.

'My visit has no special purpose. I just thought, I must discuss it with you. In the present circumstances, the Holy Church cannot keep aloof from the happenings of the world.'

The Vicar listened to him with serious attention. 'You are right,' he said. Empowered and excited by this, Mathew leaned forward and began to speak almost by way of an aside:

'Recently, someone has written that acts of violence and bloodshed as well as cries of sufferings are on the increase, despite more than one thousand million copies of the Bible being sold every year. The writer has raised a question too in the article, whether we have become complacent about this problem, trusting too much to the strength of our churches with their candles, tolling bells, and the scent of frankincense.'

Afraid he had crossed the limit, Mathew faltered. He scanned the face of the Vicar to see whether the feeling there was one of dissatisfaction, hatred, or grief.

Waking from some anxiety, the Vicar opened his eyes and looked at Mathew. Yes, he too was carried away by Mathew's words. Cutting himself off from a train of embarrassing thought, he spoke in a voice of deep concern and love for the world:

'Although the world is growing darker and darker as you have said, how can we stop believing in our little candles and our messages of love? Darkness will devour us too, unless we have faith in those things. Let us hold steadfast to our faith and keep our candles from dying in the stormy wind that breaks out. Similarly, let us preserve the scent of the frankincense from being lost and keep the sound of the church bells alive...'

The Vicar became silent for a while, as if trying to recall something.

'Sinners are multiplying before our eyes. If they confess sincerely, each will take a sitting of years... But the earth will not remain dark forever under the benign sky that glorifies God.'

He ended with a cough. Rubbing his chest, he leaned back in his chair. It was only then that Mathew noticed his senior was ill. He became perplexed and said, 'Sorry Father, I didn't know you were sick.'

'Oh, nothing to be afraid of. The winter has always been like this to me.' He sat up and his face lit up as if he were a celebrant in the altar officiating at the Eucharist.

'I think some substantial doubts still remain, don't they? But why can't you speak about them?'

Mathew twiddled his fingers on the coffee cup. The Vicar seemed willing to listen.

'Ephraim will give you some more coffee if you want.'

'No, thanks, Father.'

Mathew became voluble. Are the students, who enroll in the Apostolic Seminary, keenly aware of the things they must sacrifice in order to become priests? Does the way of celibacy, which is more sanctified and higher than married life, go with reality? How harsh are the practices used to bring them to such a disciplined faith! How cruel! How childish! A seminarian is subjected to controls and hurdles, such as warnings against girls, severe regulations about visitors, close scrutiny of incoming and outgoing letters, and the dark shadows of seminary officials escorting them and observing every movement during their rare outings. Doesn't such a candidate surrender to an inevitability, rather than choose his vocation of priesthood? Can you say that a person who embraces celibacy does it out of sincerity? At least, we must think of its impropriety. It is said that in many places the insistence on celibacy has caused a fall in the number of seminarians. Every year, about four hundred priests in America defrock themselves and abandon priesthood. Many of the churches in South America suffer from the scarcity of priests. In those churches without priests, the service is often conducted by the nuns.

With an apology, Mathew took the paper from the Vicar's hand and eagerly scanned the page for the opinion of a priest cited on celibacy. The Vicar listened carefully. 'Enforced celibacy is opposed to the very law of nature that renders life of a person incomplete without the companionship of a partner of the opposite sex.'

The priest cited in the paper added that sex was not indispensable. The temptation could be overcome. But the loneliness! That was something too difficult to get over. The priest wrote that he lived in a big building, along with a number of old as well as young priests. They scarcely spoke to one another and sometimes he wished he had someone to speak to.

'Yes, it is an unbearably painful situation. The sufferings of loneliness and inability to adapt to each other will certainly cause great difficulties. But is it a simple problem that can be resolved through marriage? In my opinion, it is sex and sex alone that makes priests want to marry.'

The Vicar added that he was in perfect agreement with the spirit of Paul VI's encyclical on celibacy. He quoted a passage from the gospel according to Matthew, in support of his position: 'There are eunuchs who have been so from birth, and there are eunuchs who have been made eunuchs by others, and there are eunuchs who have made themselves eunuchs for the sake of the kingdom of heaven.'

To this, Mathew replied, 'But scholars differ on interpretations. Some of them maintain that this passage has nothing to do with celibacy.'

'Yes, it has been variously interpreted,' agreed the Vicar. 'I think the last sentence in the passage categorically makes it clear that the best way to serve God is to lead an ascetic life in celibacy, rather than lead a married one. And remember, Paul's advice to the virgins is to remain as they are. Another verse from Matthew confirms this: "...in the resurrection they neither marry nor are given in marriage, but are like angels in heaven."'

Then Mathew said that it was not desirable to replicate heavenly manners on earth. 'The earthly rules are different. That is why Jesus never imposed celibacy on his apostles. All the apostles except John and Paul were married...'

'Think of the innumerable problems that will crop up after marriage. Will the parish put up with a situation, where the married priest and his wife daily quarrel with each other? Will anyone approach such a priest seeking comfort to their grief?'

'It doesn't have to be the case always.'

'I admit that. But still, I think that the priest doesn't need a helpmate. Sleeping with a woman will not take him anywhere. Out there in the world, battles will be fought. There will be attacks and counter attacks. Terrible famine will break out. Mankind will continue to have categories of thieves, prostitutes, and the sick. The priest is called to proclaim the glory of God to them. Suppose he is in his bedroom knowing his wife, while the people are knocking on the door, crying for help. The door will not open...'

Yakob was sitting under a tree at the foot of the hill when he saw Mathew coming downhill, looking terribly upset. He rose to his feet in deference. He appeared as still and lonely as the tree behind him. He had the yellow shawl wrapped around his shoulders. He stood leaning on the tree like a prophet.

Mathew walked listlessly, restless and uneasy. He did not know what to do or where to go. It was at this moment of indecision that his eyes fell on Yakob. He had not expected to meet him again that day.

Yakob beamed a happy smile, but did not budge. There seemed something strange about his posture. Impelled by some inner feeling, Mathew slowly walked toward Yakob, who lowered his head. Going very near him Mathew said, 'Yakob!' Yakob heard it, but he seemed not to. Nor did he raise his face. Mathew called him again.

Then Yakob said, 'Good luck to you.'

While Mathew stood awestruck, Yakob began to walk along with the cool wind.

Mathew called, 'Yakob!'

Yakob stopped. Without turning back, he said, 'Abandon your cassock here and go away, exulting and rejoicing in a festive mood. The vineyard planted by the stream will surely grow lush green.'

Mathew stood stupefied, until Yakob disappeared beyond the trees. It all seemed like a dream. The wind blew on the trees. Mathew turned to go, trying to recall Yakob's words. An extraordinary evening…an evening of riddles and questions… What did Yakob mean? What did Yakob know? Mathew became suspicious of Yakob. His face flushed in anxiety. He could not find an answer. The riddles and the questions remained. He walked slowly.

Two children came toward him, a boy and a slightly younger girl. They had incense burners in their hands.

Mathew tried in vain to recall which family they belonged to. Their coming with the censers seemed mysterious. They waved the censers toward him. They looked at him and bowed, bending their knees a little. Then they passed him on his right. Mathew stood astonished, but the children never turned back. They disappeared among the trees. Curls of smoke rose from among the trees.

And it came to pass that, resolute and having made an important decision, Mathew went to meet Annie. His heart gave a little flutter. He wondered how to introduce the subject. 'Annie,' he whispered.

Annie stifled a sob and held back her tears. The room was dimly lit. She stood behind the door to listen to him.

Mathew told her about his chance encounter with Yakob, and his strange words and behaviour. He thought of revealing to her everything that had happened that evening, but perhaps he would wait for another time. He also desisted from explaining Yakob's words. Annie would understand them on her own.

'I have decided. Tomorrow, we are leaving. I might have sought the Vicar's permission. But…' he stopped abruptly, remembering something.

'O, God!' Annie whimpered. She wanted to say so many things. She wanted to cry.

'Yes, there are two more passengers on the 10 o'clock bus to town tomorrow. They are travelling as strangers to each other, until they reach the town. From there they will board the train to a bigger town…'

Mathew told her everything. He had accepted a job as a lecturer in a government college. He had rented a small house with windows opening toward the sea. There was a beach and the ruins of an old castle.

He got up from the chair and looked into her eyes. 'Annie, are you scared?' Annie kissed him and wept.

The journey… The wheels of the bus rolled over the loose stones on the broken metal road. The stones fell sideways with a cry. The sun over the avenue trees became stronger as it climbed the sky. The grass on the hillsides swayed in the wind. The turtledoves cooed in the bamboo groves. The clouds wandered above the hills.

Crossing over the dark green valley, the bus entered a dry, rocky hillside.

The rocks were grey. Flocks of sheep grazed fearlessly among them. Black children rested in the shade of the rocks.

A clear river runs under the bridge, a bridge with most of its railings gone. Clothes in deep colours are spread in the sun on the tiny islands in the river. Children from the wind-beaten banana groves come running and lovingly wave their hands. Eager eyes watch from the palm leaf huts at the foot of the rocks. Faded flags flutter on bamboo poles. The graffiti are almost washed out. Groves of areca-nut palms flourish on either side. There are endless paddy fields and streams.

The bus became more and more crowded. Annie remembered how her heart fluttered when she saw the bus she was waiting for, far away on the west bank of the river, how she fumbled and almost fell while crossing the suspension bridge, and how her soles sweated in fear.

She had only books for that day's classes in her hands. She also had a ready answer, if someone asked her where she was going.

To get a photo taken for the hall ticket...

Nobody would suspect her as there was no photo studio in the parish. Still, her heart trembled. When the woman on her left, wearing a gold-embroidered upper cloth, asked her something, she sat with her eyes cast down. The woman wanted to know why the bus was late. The bus rumbled on.

Yohannan remembered the worn-out, tattered, dusty pair of leather slippers perched above the decayed pillar. He sat like an orphan.

The house wept silently. Its rooms were empty.

Yohannan held Annie's letter in his hands. He had found it in the evening, when he came home from school. Usually, Annie would reach home ahead of him. But on that day, the door remained closed. Finding the key on the windowsill, he opened the door without anxiety or fear. Maybe Annie was visiting Samuel Sir, or she might have gone to see Rosemary, whose sister was getting married.

Whistling to himself, Yohannan dropped his books on the chair and looked at his face in the mirror. It was bathed in sweat. He went to Annie's room for some powder. It was then that he saw on the table a folded paper addressed to 'my dear little brother'. He eagerly unfolded it. It was Annie's letter to him. Her tears had left splotches of spreading ink upon it.

Little brother, I am leaving this house without saying goodbye even to you. You are likely to see this note in the evening or in the night. By then your sister will have reached a fairly distant place. Will I ever be able to come home? I don't know. Having fallen in love with a priest, I have turned a traitor to the Holy Church. The parish will never forgive me. The parishioners will begin to blame me from tomorrow. My eyes become troubled when I think of the Vicar, Samuel Sir and Rosamma*chechi*. Where shall I go leaving them, you, and our home? No, I will never go anywhere. Mine is a dove's heart, little, light, and unable to plunge into great decisions. But, brother, I fear this love will carry me away. Like a storm, it will blow me away. Today is like no other day to me. Life will not be the same anymore. It is very late in the night. Tonight I will lie awake. I won't shut my eyes. I will sleep with my eyes open. I will weep until morning, remembering everything: our childhood days, our love, our happiness, the parish church, the holy masses, the censers sending out scented fumes, ornamental vases hanging from the roof girders, the flames of the altar candles, sacred robes, nuns, and the cemetery. O, my mind is restless. Let me stand by the window for a while… How dark it is outside! This night is unusually heavy with sorrow and fear. I will stay awake crying and praying till the morning. Outside, there are birds too, besides the darkness. Will there be birds that keep awake all night in the faraway towns? Will all the parishioners insult me? Some inner voice tells me to tear this letter to pieces, to wipe my tears, and stay here for good. I hear someone inside calling my name. I feel frightened. I wish I could clasp our mother in a tight embrace and cry my grief away. Tomorrow morning, you must go to the cemetery with some white flowers. Our mother will certainly bless me. She had the gentle heart of a little lamb. She will love me forever, I am sure. She will never hate me. When you return from the cemetery, tell our father that I fall at his feet and ask for forgiveness. And finally, you, my little brother, must forgive me…

Yohannan stood still for a fairly long time after reading the letter. Then the walls heard him crying. He sat on the floor and wept. There was no one to comfort him.

Silence was all around him. Dead silence.

The house stood as if abandoned. Within it, Yohannan was alone. He was overwhelmed with grief. He began to know himself in order to drive away his sorrow. He smelled of sweat and urine. White flowers were bursting into bloom. It was a prolonged act. He did not remember either its beginning or its end. With nowhere to go, he sat there emptily.

There prevailed a deathly silence when Thoma came home at dusk. There was neither sound nor movement. He called out to Annie. But she did not respond. He was going to remove his shirt. But, hearing no sound from inside, even though the door was open, he became suspicious and went in immediately. There was no one in the kitchen. The back door was closed. There was no fire in the hearth. There was no sign that said Annie had ever entered the kitchen this evening. Where had she gone?

Worried, Thoma went to Annie's room. He saw Yohannan lying curled on the floor beneath the cupboard. Going near, he called him and hunched beside him. He touched him on the shoulder. Yohannan woke up frightened. He sat up hurriedly, when he saw his father.

'What happened? What is the problem?' Thoma asked.

Yohannan did not speak. Raising his voice, Thoma enquired about Annie.

'*Chechi* went away,' he whimpered.

'Where?' he asked.

Yohannan gave Annie's letter to him. Standing by the window, he quickly read it through. He tore the letter to pieces and went out. Yohannan did not ask him where he was going. He got up, went to the door and saw his father hurrying away. He guessed he was going to meet the Vicar.

Yes, it was to the Vicar that Thoma went. The Vicar had been informed of everything by Mathew in a note he had sent through a parishioner returning from town.

After a long silence, Thoma lost patience and asked, 'Why don't you say anything, Father?'

The Vicar had nothing to say.

Angrily, Thoma walked out. The Vicar went after him to the door and wanted to call out to him. But he could not. Thoma would not have stopped, even if he had been called.

Thoma walked steadily. He did not notice either the dry wind blowing, or the night falling. He did not see Yakob coming straight toward him. Yakob stood on the roadside watching him carefully. He smiled to himself, showing all his teeth. He neither stopped Thoma, nor did he follow him. Thoma walked along the footpath. A pig trotted behind him. It was a big, fat pig, with an especially charming tread. Its skin was fair and its little tail moved rhythmically with its steps.

Hearing a noise, Thoma turned back and saw the pig. When he stopped, the pig also stopped. What! He stood aside.

Wagging its tail, the pig stood still and looked at Thoma.

Thoma raised his hand to frighten the pig. But the pig only twitched its legs and refused to run away. He bent down for a stone and threw it at the pig.

The pig ran away grunting, leaving him behind.

Thoma saw the pig disappear in the thickening darkness. But he did not realize that it was his own pig.

One more April has come to pass. No sooner do you wave the censer than the fume loses its scent in the dusty wind. The stones crackle in the cries of the yellow leaves and the withered roots. This month of April is like the longest sigh ever…

The school final exam is over. Annie had written to him to work hard and secure a first class.

'Here, the college is near the house. You can stay with us and go to college. I am thinking of going to college next year. Otherwise, I get bored during the day. We can go together.'

Annie has found happiness in life.

Her occasional letters bear the glow and warmth of her joy. I wish her all the best, thought Yohannan.

The exams are over. I don't think I will pass. Father did not ask me anything. Nor did I tell him anything. All the teachers say that Joshi will pass with a first class.

I feel a little jealous of Joshi, who sits in the examination hall and eagerly fills pages and pages. When he forgets something, he sits for a while, eyes fixed on the wall, holding the pen against his lips, trying to recollect what he has forgotten, and then bends his head and writes hurriedly.

The wind blew over his hair. Yohannan ran his fingers over his upper lip, watching Joshi's trembling hair. He had forgotten all the answers. He looked indifferently at the questions and the answer book full of corrections and lines scored out. At times, he deliberately wrote stupidities. Every day, he left the examination hall quite listlessly. On the last day of exams, Joshi said that he would pass with fairly good marks, provided he had God's grace. If he passed, he would enroll in a theological college in some faraway town.

Perhaps, after several years, we will meet here, thought Yohannan. I will be here on this side of the confessional. You will be the Father confessor. You will hear my confession. I will tell you how fervently I loved you and how many nights I imagined you were sleeping with me. I will confess all my sins to you. We shall meet.

You are still with me now. Let me recollect the hair coming before your eyes, your eyebrows seeming to meet, the redness of your lips, and your sparkling smile. Joshi, my beloved, I will not forget you. I will include this too in my confession.

My eyes have become slightly reddened. They seem to have blurred. The mirror is darkening all over. My face! My smell!

Annie, Samuel Sir died two days ago. I heard the bell when I was lying down to sleep at night. I was alone in the house. Father has been away somewhere for two days. Perhaps, he is in the hills. When I heard the bell, I shut the door and went to Samuel Sir's house. He was dead before I reached his house. I attended the funeral. I had visited him two weeks before he died. I could hardly recognize him then. He was so changed. When he saw me, his eyes filled with tears. I sat there and wept. I don't understand why God has meted out so much suffering to him. I have pondered upon this question many times. I don't know the answer. I could not control my grief, when I followed his hearse in the funeral procession in the night. The sky was full of stars. The cemetery was full of people. Samuel Sir came from the dust, he returned to the dust. Over his coffin, I offered an extra pinch of dust on your behalf. When I came home from the burial, to tell you the truth, I was overcome by fear. There was not a single soul nearby, save the pig in the sty. By the by, our big pig has been missing since the day you left. Either it ran away into the hills or someone has secretly killed and eaten it. There is only one pig left in the sty. I held on to the plank of the sty and looked at it. I think I babbled to it. I don't remember anything. I lay there until morning. I felt I was an orphan. With the death of Samuel Sir, I feel all the more lonely. Perhaps that's how it should be.

Yesterday, I went to Samuel Sir's house. It was not a planned visit. Walking purposelessly, I ended up there. Rosamma*chechi* was sitting on the veranda. Though she looked at me, she did not seem to see anything. She appeared so weak, as if she had suddenly turned very old. I had no words to console her. I turned and walked away silently. What is here to sustain her? Who is here to support her?

The summer is over and gone. The rainy season has set in. The cassava flourishes on the slopes. The wayside trees are washed clean of dust. It is dark green all around. The river bank is thick with grass.

Yohannan walked leisurely, waving a blade of grass. Evening was darkening over the river, the *aattuvanchi* leaves, and the meadows. The quails were twittering in the thickets.

He had bathed in the morning. He could take a dip in the river now, but he did not have a bath towel. If he had been wearing a shirt, it would have served the purpose. Standing in the tall grass he thought of going home and returning with a towel. Then Rahel came that way.

She had been bathing in the river. She carried her wet clothes on her left arm. Waving her hair dry with her right hand, she came near Yohannan.

'Are you going to bathe?' Rahel asked.

'Yes,' he blurted.

'But you have no bath towel.'

'No, I'm just walking.'

When Rahel was about to walk past him, Yohannan enquired, 'Rahel, will you pass your exams?'

She smiled to herself, pushing her wet hair back from her chest.

'I don't know. What about you?'

'O, I didn't write anything to pass.'

His eyes fell on Rahel, when he said this. Drops of water here and there glistened on her neck. Her rose-coloured jacket was wet. Her breasts were small. His eyes went piercing through her clothes. They were very near; so near that he could reach out and touch them. Still, Rahel had that charming smile to herself on her lips.

Driven by some sudden impulse, Yohannan drew her close to him. Bewildered, she was about to call his name, when he pulled her down into the grass. He pressed his lips on her forehead and cheeks. Rahel wriggled under him and said, 'No.' Then his lips knew her lips. Her lower lip twitched between his lips. He felt its wetness and the warmth of the blood inside. He ran his fingers along her sleek, throbbing neck. His searching fingers wandered over her wet jacket and felt all her distress. She was crying. His eyes also became wet. He was about to say something, but could not think of words. He ran his fingers over Rahel's body with a wordless whimper. His hand quivered, as if feverish. His hand moved like a lament, like a psalm chanted mournfully.

Later, Yohannan knew he was waking up from a sleep.

He woke up in the lush grass on the riverside. He wondered how he came there. He did not know. He lay on his side. Suddenly, he remembered Rahel. He remembered meeting her and speaking to her on the way. Then he sat up. Chewing a blade of grass, he tried to remember. Was it all a fantasy or reality?

In the middle of the thickets, Yakob distilled his arrack. As he sat on his knees, puffing at the fire, he did not hear Yohannan approaching and retreating stealthily.

Yohannan wandered into the cashew grove. It was like a paradise. The wind blew full blast. He strolled under the trees, sucking the juice of a fruit plucked from a low branch. His feet became cool, walking on shadow after shadow. He himself moved like a pale shadow through the smell of cashew fruits.

There was a road that ran between the cashew grove and the rubber plantation. Circling a meadow and passing through the woods, it continued toward the eastern hills past the plantation and the grove.

When he came near the bamboo cluster at the end of the plantation, Yohannan saw a line of crosses approaching at a distance. He was amazed. Hiding behind the bamboos, he peeped toward the road.

The atonement procession was approaching. The Vicar was at the head of the procession, holding a cross. Behind him, in double line, the children and the grownups of the parish followed, each carrying a cross.

They held the crosses high as they walked. The body and face of the Vicar were covered in dust. His feet and the tip of his cassock were reddened with dust. He puffed and panted up the climbs and down the descents. The children followed close behind. They walked silently, occasionally looking at the sky above and the crosses in their hands.

Yohannan saw Rahel among the girls.

Rahel looked pale. She wore a blue skirt with white borders and a light blue jacket. On her neck was a string of white stones. Her curly hair was neatly combed. She held the cross with both hands.

Yohannan felt deep regret and turned his face. Yakob was standing behind him.

Yohannan was shocked beyond expression. His regret for Rahel went to pieces, like a dried leaf chips away.

Yakob waited till the atonement procession passed. His

face was taut with inner disturbance. His eyes seemed lost among faraway things.

As the pilgrims trudged along the red road, Yakob turned his back, making a sound of disgust. He furrowed his eyebrows, as if the procession was improper. Yohannan understood his contempt and displeasure.

'Bold headlines will appear in the newspapers: An atonement procession for the welfare and development of the parish,' Yakob said sarcastically. 'Well, well, and a photograph of parishioners marching and carrying crosses, ha-ha.' With a guffaw, he walked toward the cashew trees.

Yohannan did not know what to do. The last shadow had vanished from the path. Only the footprints remained.

Yohannan got up and followed Yakob, as if walking in his sleep.

Yakob was still muttering in contempt. Occasionally, he smiled to himself.

'Yes, we need things like this.' Yohannan heard when he was near.

Yohannan paused.

'You didn't go?' Yakob asked.

'No.'

'No one should keep away, when atonement of sin is sought.'

Yohannan felt a little bold. 'What about Yakob*chettan*?'

'Ha, ha… I don't know what sin is, child. I don't know which activities come under sin.'

'Sin,' Yohannan whispered.

'A meaningless word,' added Yakob.

He started to walk. Yohannan followed him.

'You know, the priests keep repeating this word. Probably this is the word they use most. O, how this small word resounds! Only three letters! But it has an unusual majesty and resonance about it!'

It seemed to Yohannan that Yakob was muttering from another world. Following Yakob, he held on to a branch and climbed down the terrace.

'Sit here. I will pour you a little.'

'Oh, no, I don't want to drink.'

'You are no longer a little baby.'

Yohannan was scared.

'I am going.'

'Are you going to the procession?'

Yohannan did not reply.

'Sit here.'

Yohannan sat, quite unnerved. After puffing it cool, Yakob held the arrack toward Yohannan.

'I made this for my own use, not for sale. It is excellent stuff and nothing to fear.'

He swallowed a little arrack. It burned his throat as it went down. In the confusion, he bent forward.

'Don't mind. Close your eyes and drink it in one swallow.'

Yohannan shook his head, but his refusal was weak.

When he finished it, he belched. His head shuddered. Something was echoing inside it.

'Light a beedi. A beedi goes well with arrack.'

Yohannan did not hesitate. He took one from the packet Yakob held out and put it to his lips.

Lifting a firebrand from the fire, Yakob lighted it.

Yohannan puffed out the smoke and fluttered his eyes. He saw a cross, and behind it…

He leaned back a little. I am touching a moist lip. Two teats become taut at the touch of my fingertip. A navel throbs. A lower abdomen quivers.

His head became heavy. He fell down as if hit by a cloud. Then Yakob said, fixing his eyes far away, 'It is necessary to put an end to this. Because…'

Yohannan did not hear the rest of what he said.

Yohannan turned and looked. Sitting in Lohitakshan's barbershop, postman Peter was calling him. Perhaps, there was a letter from Annie.

When he hurried into the shop, Peter said, 'There is no letter. I called you to ask you about Yakob. Have you seen him anywhere?'

'No.'

'Lohitakshan says he has not been here for two days. Nor is he in his house.'

'I saw him the day before yesterday,' said Yohannan.

'Where?'

Suddenly, Yohannan felt foolish to have said it. Now he could not evade them.

'Yakob*chettan* was on the riverside, below the Pathippally family's cashew grove.'

'He must have been making arrack?'

'Yes.' Yohannan bent his head.

He remembered how the Pathippally cashew grove suddenly darkened and he fell down. Yakob*chettan* talked about putting an end to something…

Night was almost falling when I awoke. I lay still for some time with my eyes open. The sky above stood like a sentinel.

I came round little by little. Yakob*chettan* was lying asleep nearby. I shook him and called once or twice. He did not hear.

I struggled to sit upright. My head ached.

Rising to my feet, I thought I might fall, but I stumbled home. Yakob*chettan* was lying asleep on the grass and dirt.

'O, then he must be sleeping, after having drunk his fill,' said Peter.

'Will he still be there?' wondered Yohannan.

'That guy is used to sleeping at a stretch for two days. He won't even move in between.'

'No one can say anything for certain about him,' added Lohitakshan.

'I suppose, he must be there. Let me go and look.'

Peter invited Yohannan to come along. As he had no customers waiting, Lohitakshan also accompanied them. They met Philipos on the way. When he knew where they were going, he joined them.

When they went and looked, Yakob was still asleep.

They soon realized that he would never wake up.

Yohannan mourned Yakob for many days. Yakob went his way, he thought. His heart wept sore remembering him.

Lohitakshan's scissors moved very fast over the hair of Philipos, who dozed in his chair in blissful forgetfulness. Behind them sat Yohannan, reading a film magazine. In fact, he was looking at the pictures in it. Pictures of cine actresses, carefully cut out from magazines, were stuck all over the walls.

Lohitakshan, having finished the haircut, called Philipos many times, before he opened his eyes on the picture of an actress in a bikini. Philipos peered at his own reflection through the many splotches on the ancient mirror.

'Oh, finished? I suppose, I slept a little.'

'*Chettan*, here, please hold your face straight.'

Lohitakshan took a syringe-shaped bottle to spray water on his customer's face.

'No need of that.'

'You cannot say that. This is part of the ritual,' said Lohitakshan. Then he sprayed water thrice on his face. Each time Philipos shut his eyes tight and flinched.

Taking a towel from his shoulder, Lohitakshan wiped Philipos's face. Then he sprinkled powder plentifully upon his face and the nape of his neck. The sharp scent of the powder rose all around them.

When he realized that Lohitakshan's rituals were over, Philipos struggled to his feet. He stared at his image in the mirror as if he suspected it to be somebody else.

'Hooom!' Taking money out from his pocket, he counted it and gave it to Lohitakshan. Lohitakshan humbly put it in his pocket, without checking how much it was.

As Philipos turned once again to the mirror, trying to recognize his own image, Yohannan rose to his feet with agitation, putting aside the weekly he had been reading.

'Crop or shave?' Lohitakshan asked.

Yohannan, who was about to sit, looked about timidly to see if Philipos had left. To his relief, Philipos was beyond earshot, talking with postman Peter.

Yohannan observed his own face in the mirror. There were brown hairs growing on his chin as well as below his nose. In a single breath he said, 'Both...'

Then he worried what would happen, if somebody else came in before his haircut and shave were done. Perhaps Peter*chettan* would engage them with his idle talk. Anyway, it had been decided, and he must sit through it indifferently.

As if enacting a ritual, Lohitakshan wrapped the towel around Yohannan's neck and shoulders. He sat there looking carefully at his own reflection.

Lohitakshan's relevance in the life of the parish is evident in the relatively innocent and uncomplicated question, 'Crop or shave?' If Lohitakshan were memorable as a mere barber, then why don't the parishioners remember Vasudevan, who was very vocal about the rights and demands of barbers as a social minority? Vasudevan, who fell in love with a girl in a circus troupe that visited the parish one December, left the parish along with the troupe. No one here remembers Vasudevan. His barbershop, plastered with posters demanding the abolition of contract labour and the permanent appointment of barbers in government departments of health and police, collapsed one monsoon season. No one noticed. No one complained about it.

But the boys in the parish will never forget Lohitakshan. He establishes the closest relation with them. When he finds the children have grown to a certain level—this knowledge is undoubtedly important—he begins to speak to them about girls. It is from him that they learn to look at girls in a new way. He knows all their secrets. He knows exactly how much they've grown. He knows that one of the most decisive moments in the life of a boy starts with the question, 'Crop or shave?'

The scissors continued to snip. Lohitakshan looked indifferently at the hair. The hair surrendered to the scissors.

'Lohitakshan, give this to the Panthackal children if they come.' Peter held out a letter without climbing up to the shop.

Scouring his portfolio, he fished out some more letters.

'There is a letter without a receiver in today's post,' said Peter.

'Who is the letter for?

'To our Yakob.'

Lohitakshan laughed. Though he laughed gently, it would have been better, if he had not laughed at all, Yohannan thought. Then Peter joined in. Yohannan wished that at least Peter had not laughed.

'Look there, they are carrying Sara's husband.' Peter announced.

'Philipos*chettan* said they were taking him to the hospital.'

'He is sinking.'

'Yes.'

'He is going to escape.'

'What about her?'

Turning his head, Yohannan looked toward the road. Four people were carrying Skaria on a coir bed. Skaria was wrapped in a blanket from head to foot. Only his face was uncovered. It moved from side to side with the movement of the coir bed. Yohannan wondered whether he was lying with his eyes shut. Or, perhaps, eyes wide open, he might be enjoying his last view of the sky. He might be watching every cloud moving, the blue slopes appearing occasionally among the clouds, and the birds flapping their wings. He will not see the sky again in a similar journey like this. Above him, a plank will hide the sky from his view. Even if his eyes are open, the sky will be alien to him.

The Skaria crowd went along, silently. Lagging behind them was Sara, her head covered with a sari, in deep sorrow. Sara was alone.

When they disappeared from sight, Peter said, 'Sara's condition is pitiable. I don't think Skaria will see the hospital. What will happen to her? She has no children.'

'What of that? Can't she get married again? Isn't it convenient that she has no children?'

'Yes, but it is not that easy.'

'Sara has an elder sister somewhere.'

'Yes, Katrina. I know.'

'She can sell her property here and go to her.

'Yes, but I fear Sara won't go anywhere.'

'That's what you wish.'

'Ha, ha. You have found it out.'

'Beware. Our Yakob*chettan* will come from his grave and threaten you.'

'What! He won't give up Sara, even after death?'

'That's it.'

'Alas!'

'He will loiter there.'

'Nothing doing.'

'But he won't concede.'

'Then who will do justice to Sara as he wished? Who will rectify God's mistake and love her?'

'Are you suggesting that you love her?'

'What is this love if not what a man and woman do together after undressing?'

'Ha, ha!'

Lohitakshan laughed aloud. Arranging the letters in his portfolio, Peter got ready to leave. The umbrella with the cane handle hung from the back of his collar. The soles of his shoes were almost worn out.

'Is there any news from your sister Annie?' Lohitakshan asked Yohannan.

Thinking of something else, Yohannan did not hear him. He awoke, startled.

'What?'

'Your sister...'

'What about my sister?

'...is clever.'

Jumping out of the chair, Yohannan turned and slapped Lohitakshan's cheek. Lohitakshan fell backward against the wall.

Yohannan whipped the towel from his neck and threw it at Lohitakshan.

'How dare you say anything about my sister?' He was trembling with rage.

Climbing down to the road, Yohannan muttered, 'Son of a bitch.'

Lohitakshan rose to his feet as Yohannan started to walk away. Dropping the scissors and the comb on the floor, he also climbed down the steps.

'Hey, you! Stop!'

Yohannan turned and stopped.

Lohitakshan caught up with him and hit him hard on his face. Yohannan turned and caught Lohitakshan by the throat. They fell and tumbled about in the gravel.

The Vicar and his sexton were passing by and happened to see it.

'What is happening there?' the Vicar asked.

The sexton ran toward them and was eager to separate them.

'Isn't it Yohannan?'

Yohannan raised his face. But suddenly, he dropped it.

Lohitakshan rose to his feet and dusted the sand and gravel from his body.

'Yohannan, get up,' the Vicar said calmly.

Yohannan slowly rose to his feet. He did not bother to dust himself off. He stood as if frightened, staring at the ground.

'What was the quarrel about?' the sexton asked.

With a gesture of his hand, the Vicar silenced him; he touched Yohannan on the shoulder and said, 'Walk, I'm also going your way.'

When Yohannan woke up in the morning, his body ached all over. He lay there thinking of the night.

He stared at the four walls and the roof.

The walls and the roof looked at him. His face was overcome by gloom.

The results of the school final exams were published. Having failed, Jessy Abraham was on the verge of tears, when some girls took her to the backyard of the school to sit her down, to console her. With an ironic smile, Yohannan stood on the veranda. But Joshi did not join him.

'How can you smile?' Joshi asked.

'Is failing an exam a grievous matter?'

'I don't know.'

Joshi had passed with a first class. Yohannan had failed miserably.

Jessy Abraham went on crying. Failure was the cause of her sorrow. Her heart melted and became like water.

'You should have studied,' Joshi said to Yohannan.

'Perhaps…'

'The exam was not very difficult.'

'Yes.'

'Appear for the supplementary exam in September and secure a first class.'

'Let me see.'

They strolled along the veranda aimlessly, silently. When they reached the end, they stopped. Yohannan looked into Joshi's eyes.

'Can't you refuse to join the seminary?' Yohannan asked, on the verge of tears.

Joshi turned his face away. Holding him by the shoulder, Yohannan turned Joshi toward him.

Again, he looked at Joshi with the most aching eyes on earth.

'Can't you get out of it?'

'No,' Joshi said, like a deep sigh.

One morning, Joshi left for the seminary. It rained steadily as he started from home and as he waited for the bus. Yohannan could not make out clearly what Joshi said while boarding the bus.

Sitting in a window seat, he lifted the tarpaulin curtain and looked out through the rain.

Yohannan saw him through the rain.

The rain stood between them.

They neither smiled, nor cried. The rain went on pouring between them.

All of Joshi's people had come to see him off. There were Agnes, Susan, and Valsamma. They heartily wished him well. Esther stretched her hand toward her son. By then, the bus had started moving. Daniel, sitting by his side, gently detached Joshi's hand and dropped the curtain.

Esther and her daughters did not say anything. Yohannan said, 'I'm going.'

Esther invited him to their house. She said they had expected him on the previous night.

Yes. I came as expected. But no one saw me. Mother and Agnes were busy packing Joshi's things. Joshi was talking to Susan and Valsamma. They all smiled, though with pain. They all fell silent when Daniel, sitting a little apart, began to read the holy book in a heavy voice. Gradually, their eyes filled with tears. I pressed my handkerchief hard over my mouth. My weeping and wailing was stifled. It was unbearable. The floor, where my feet rested, and the wall, on which my body leaned, were rough.

The night was dark. There was no other way except sinning to myself, I thought. So I sinned to myself.

'Last night, he wept,' said Valsamma.

'I, too, heard it,' Susan said.

'I too,' said Esther.

'But Mother, you didn't say anything,' Agnes said sadly.

'I told your father. He said, he, too, had heard it. When we went to look, we found our son had lowered the wick of the lamp and was kneeling in prayer.

Yohannan remembered: Not my will, but thine.

Yohannan again remembered: Go to the city that has foundations.

He does not know where it is. But Joshi will probably reach there. He will raise his voice to God and praise him. He will fear no one. His heart will remain steadfast. His songs of praise will make the meadows and paths overflow with bounty. The hills will gird themselves with joy. The pastures will fill themselves with flocks. The valleys will cover themselves with grain.

They walked sluggishly along the foot of the hill, as if it were a time of mourning. It was drizzling. The hill and the footpaths were soaking wet. The leaves stood clean.

When they were near their home, the dog came panting to the road to meet them. He searched for someone among Esther and her children.

'Poor dog, he also wanted to come,' said Esther. 'We didn't take him along, as there was nobody to keep watch of the house. He seems unhappy.' The dog walked alongside them. Coffee and red chilly grew on either side of the road. Rows of pineapple were planted close to the threshing floor. The house stood overlooking a meadow.

It was a small house built of baked bricks. At the door were a crucifix with the crown of thorns, a Christmas card, and a picture of Mary's sacred heart. A family photo hung on the right. Esther, Daniel, and Joshi are sitting on chairs in the front row. Agnes, Susan, and Valsamma are standing behind them. There is a look of amazement on the faces of Valsamma and Susan. Agnes, putting on a veil, has a gentle smile on her lips. Esther and Daniel are sitting in tranquil silence. On their left sits Joshi in a manner revealing the purity of his heart. His eyes are shining. There is a thin cascade of hair on his forehead. He holds a Bible piously, pressing it to his chest.

As he stood there, looking at the photograph, Yohannan's eyes became troubled. He sat on the cot. When the dog came and sat at his feet, looking up to his face, he tried to be friendly. But the dog left him, making muttering sounds, and lay curled in a corner.

'He was very close to our brother,' said Agnes.

'When is he coming home?' asked Yohannan.

'He may be coming for the vacation.'

Yohannan went in and looked around in Joshi's room. Joshi still seemed to be on his knees in the middle of the room. His lips trembled. His eyes were streaming.

Yohannan recalled: Not my will but thine be done.

'Come, son,' Esther called from behind. She held a plate of sliced pineapple.

He sat with a bowed head. The pineapple was as sweet as honey.

'What about Annie?' Esther enquired, sitting by his side on the coir bed.

'O, she is well.'

'Does she send letters?'

'Yes, she does occasionally.'

'Does she write to your father?'

'Yes. But he does not read them. He is still angry with her.'

'Poor child.'

Yohannan looked at her face. Esther closed her eyes in a prayer. Yohannan saw pigeons in the courtyard. The pigeons saw Yohannan on the veranda.

Susan brought a notebook from the cupboard in the room and showed it to Yohannan. It was full of pictures drawn by Joshi. Yohannan looked at the pictures. Esther crossed herself.

After the rain, the sun shone bright over the parish. The trees and the roofs dried out. By evening, a cool wind began to blow. But there were no rain clouds in the sky. It was raining somewhere else.

Yohannan did not want to leave them. Where should he go? Should he go to an empty house? But he could not stay here. Yohannan left them under the pretext of some urgent task. At a fairly good distance, he turned and saw them all beyond the coffee plants. Yohannan felt a sob heaving from his heart. Then he walked aimlessly and listlessly, looking down at his feet. It seemed meaningless to him. He wanted to toss his umbrella into the thickets or among the rocks. But the umbrella, in panic, shrank into his hands. Climbing on a rock, he urinated for a long time. He wished it would never end. But unfortunately, it ended. Then keep walking, he muttered to himself.

To distract himself, he turned his attention to the roads. It was along a road cut through the hillside that he was walking. It was made by breaking away rocks. Circling the hill, it goes downhill. Many footpaths lead to it. Or is it the other way? Do the footpaths lead to it or do they depart from it? Not quite sure. They lead to houses, rubber trees, bamboo clusters, and the riverside. Separate paths go to the sexton's house, the blacksmith's compound, and the bootlegger's hide-out. There is only one road to the butcher who sells pork and beef.

How many roads, big and small, there are in this parish, Yohannan wondered. Through them, you can leave. But you only arrive at another parish.

Yohannan felt like whistling. And he did whistle.

The house was empty still. Taking the key from the top of the pillar, he opened the door. Later he felt it was no use opening the door. Yesterday, they had run out of rice. Father is not in the habit of storing things. I must go to Baby*chettan*'s shop with the credit book. There, we can purchase rice and groceries, and meet people. Anyway, I cannot go there today. Let it be tomorrow. Father may come home boozy and quarrel with me. Or he may not come. He is also likely to fall asleep on the veranda of the liquor shop or at somebody else's house. It all depends on Father's convenience. Yohannan came out and stood in the courtyard. The pigsty too was empty. There was no hope of the sty ever being filled with pigs. But it seemed to him that the sty was full of pigs writhing, and that they were all grunting.

Then Rahel came.

Rahel came with her goats. The goats stood between Rahel and Yohannan. Unable to look Rahel in the face, Yohannan looked at the goats. One kid rubbed against his legs. It tried to say something. But it stopped with a sorrowful cry.

The sunlight faded and the hilltops began to darken. The trees were bathed in the glow of the setting sun.

Yohannan's eyes wandered over the pleats of Rahel's skirt. It was the colour of leaves. Her white blouse was damp with sweat. The jingle of her bangles announced even the slightest movement of her hands.

'I would like a word with you.'

Yohannan wondered what Rahel wanted to tell him.

One of the goats bleated. Yohannan and Rahel looked at it. The smell of goats filled the air between them.

Forgetting what she wanted to say, Rahel asked him, 'Can I have Annie's address?'

Wondering why Rahel wanted Annie's address, Yohannan went inside to write it down on a piece of paper. Since he could not remember the house number and pin-code, he searched for Annie's latest letter. He had kept it in the Bible, in the second letter of St. Paul to the Thessalonians. When Yohannan ferreted out Annie's letter from the second letter of St. Paul to the Thessalonians, Rahel's shadow moved at the door.

She went near Yohannan.

'Give it to me, if it is not confidential.'

He had no objection to Rahel's reading it.

Taking Annie's letter from his hand, Rahel began to read it. In it, Annie had written that she was expecting:

My God, I am really frightened. I went to the doctor with vomiting and anaemia. How embarrassed we were when the doctor told us with a quizzical smile to 'get ready to welcome a guest into the family!'

Rahel continued to read the letter with a shy little smile. Her face became sympathetic when she came toward the end:

I am worried only about you. When I sit down to eat, I forget my hunger wondering whether you have prepared anything to eat. Little one, you come and stay with us, though it is already late...

Rahel looked at Yohannan with sympathy.

Yohannan was standing by the window, trying to see something outside.

Rahel went near him and, a bit hesitatingly, touched him on the shoulder. Suddenly, he began to sob, pressing his face to the window. Rahel was bewildered. When she held his shoulder and turned him toward her, he fell into her arms and cried. He pressed his face on her small breasts. She caressed his hair and back. He held her tight, fearing that she would go away at any moment. When he lifted his face, he found Rahel's cheeks were wet. Her lips trembled. Crying, he kissed her. 'Don't cry,' Rahel told him.

They became naked. But they were not ashamed. They lay in the dust. They lay fallen in the dust.

Rahel felt it was very late. She said, 'I must go.'

'Why?'

Looking at him, Rahel pitied him.

The goats were waiting for her outside. When she was on the veranda, Yohannan told her to stop. He went inside and returned with Annie's letter. He held it to her. Without saying anything, Rahel took it and stepped into the courtyard.

The goats were impatient. They bleated when they saw her. She walked two steps with the goats and stopped. Yohannan was standing close to the pillar on the veranda.

Rahel felt pity for Yohannan. She came this way to tell him something. She need not do that anymore, she thought.

Yohannan stood looking at Rahel's face. She has seen my affliction; she has heard my cry, he thought.

It was night. In his room, Yohannan sat beside the lamp. His eyes were in the *Book of Leviticus*. Jehovah again went on speaking to Moses and Aaron.

Yohannan expected Rahel the next day, in the evening. But neither she, nor the goats came that way. On that day, the parish suddenly became darkened. Thoma came tottering from somewhere. When he heard the sound, Yohannan came out to the veranda, holding the hurricane lamp. His father's face appeared in the light of the lamp. Raising his face once, Thoma dismissed him with a gesture of his hand. Yohannan went back to his room, without waiting to say anything. A little later, he could hear snoring from the veranda. He turned to himself for a companion. The body and face of Rahel came alive in memory. He knew himself, as if it were Rahel. He desecrated his body until next evening.

Rahel did not come the next day either. He decided to go and look for her.

Climbing the wooded terraces at the back of his house, Yohannan walked toward Rahel's house. He heard the bleating of a goat from somewhere. It drew him closer to Rahel's memory. He grew anxious whether she would be home. Perhaps—

Anyway, I should go and look, he decided. He walked past the trees. The sunlight was gone. It seems it is about to rain. The clouds are darkening above the hills. I can hear the prayer from the church. It was a long time since he had attended the holy mass, he thought. What shall I say when I see the Vicar? This thought pressed on him. He quivered, as if hit by the rainy wind. When he saw the hills, the woods, and the clouds, he felt he was alone among them. Besides, if it rains too—

When he was near Rahel's house, he hesitated and stopped. He heard voices of children from beyond the yam and cassava beds. Seeing Yohannan, a timid dog in the courtyard barked. Shiny called the dog away. Silvy came out into the veranda to see who it was.

'Where is your father?' asked Yohannan.

'He hasn't come,' said Shiny and Silvy simultaneously.

Wiping both her hands on her soiled lungi, Rahel's mother came to the door.

'Who is this here?'

Yohannan smiled.

'I was just passing.'

Yohannan looked to see whether Rahel was standing behind the door.

'George*chettan* didn't come, did he?'

'No. Did you know about it?'

Yohannan was confused.

'No.'

'He and Rahel went yesterday morning.'

'Where did they go?' Yohannan asked in a hurry.

'To admit her in the convent.' Rahel's mother said this like a sigh and leaned her head against the door frame. Yohannan became pale. He looked toward the house and longed to cry aloud. Shiny and Silvy were staring at him as if they were frightened. Behind them was the weary face of Rahel's mother. The house inside was full of darkness. The prayer from the church had ended.

The moment he learned Rahel was gone, Yohannan felt like an old man with one foot in the grave. He wanted to totter to the church and ring the bell to tell all the parishioners his tragedy. He did not notice anyone who passed him. People were hurrying home from work. Nobody knew what had happened to Yohannan. Perhaps they would never know it. Yohannan walked along with a mind full of emptiness and sorrow.

He was as lonely as a solitary bird. Even his shadow did not accompany him. The parish had become darkened with low, heavy rain clouds, and the day was almost ending. On the crest of the hill, standing in deep meditation, a cross could be seen against the dark clouds.

The Vicar, strolling in the church courtyard, called Ephraim and told him, it was going to rain.

When Ephraim came out, it had already started drizzling. The Vicar still paced, his hands clasped behind him over his long cassock.

'Father, this is too much,' Ephraim scolded mildly.

The Vicar replied, 'Ephraim, this is not a hailstorm.'

The drizzle began to fall on the cemetery like tears.

When Ephraim complained, 'Father, what will happen, if you act like a little child?', the Vicar got into the veranda, thinking it pointless to argue with him. Without bothering to wipe away the raindrops from his face, he leaned on the pillar, looking at the courtyard and down into the valley.

Then he saw a woman, drenched in rain, climbing uphill to the church. He looked eagerly to the road to see who it was. She was in white. Her head was covered with the end of her sari.

'Ephraim, do you know who is coming uphill?' the Vicar asked.

Ephraim observed her for some time and said, 'Father, it is Sara.'

Sara, with a weeping and wailing heart, indifferent to the pouring rain.

It was not rain, but tears, that the Vicar saw on her face. He heaved a sigh, wondering how to console Sara, who was kneeling before him.

Sara was crying.

'Father, I am abandoned. I am left alone.'

'Why do you say that?' Lifting his hands upwards, the Vicar said in a faltering voice, 'His mercy will never end. Keep hope. Lift your arms in prayer.'

'There is no sorrow like my sorrow,' Sara wept.

'Sara, wait here till the rain is over.'

She stood for a moment hesitating. Then, without lifting her face, she turned, saying, 'I'm going.'

'Then, take an umbrella.' The Vicar called Ephraim and told him to bring an umbrella.

When Ephraim came back with the umbrella, the Vicar stood, looking pale, and Sara was walking away in the rain.

Climbing downhill, Sara passed Yohannan. After leaving Rahel's house, he too was walking aimlessly in the rain, feeling the distress of a dying old man. His heart was full of emptiness and sorrow. He remembered seeing a cross against the dark clouds. The cross was on the crest of the hill that stood as if in deep meditation. On a sudden whim, he had thought of going to the church and ringing the bell to tell his pain to all the parishioners. Perhaps, it had occurred to him, before his eyes were drawn to the cross.

Where? How far yet to go? When he raised his face in distress, he saw Sara in front of him. By then, the rain had become heavier. It was too heavy to go without an umbrella. But they did not care. Sara saw him and went past, covering her head with the end of her sari, which she held with both hands.

Standing stock still in the rain, Yohannan watched Sara. While he wondered why Sara was walking alone in the rain, he heard Ephraim's complaint:

'How awfully fast she walks! How can this old man keep pace with her? If I go back without giving the umbrella to her, the Father will not like it.'

Complaining thus to himself, Ephraim came near Yohannan.

'Hey, why have you stopped dead here in this pouring rain?'

A lightning smile shone and flitted across Yohannan's wet face.

'Excellent.'

'What happened to her?' Yohannan asked, turning his face in the direction Sara went.

'Didn't you know, son? Her husband died yesterday in some hospital somewhere. They buried him there. She is on her way home.'

Ephraim walked away hurriedly with the umbrella for Sara, feeling guilty for having stopped to speak that much to him.

'Go to the church. The Father is there.' Ephraim said as he went.

Yohannan did not hear Ephraim. He was thinking of Sara's lot. He understood the sorrow of Sara, who walked alone and drenched in rain, with no one to go with her. He remembered how four people had carried Skaria on a coir bed. The carriers might have returned with the empty bed after boarding him in a bus. Sitting in the bus, coughing and croaking, Skaria might have reached the town. Alighting slowly, leaning on Sara's shoulder—

They must have sounded the church bell, announcing Skaria's death. I might have been sleeping then, thought Yohannan.

Soaking wet, he shuddered. He sought refuge under the heavy canopy of a roadside tree. He looked at the rain falling on the distant hills and woods.

This rain may be falling outside Rahel's window. What might be the colour of that window? Yellow? Blue? Perhaps it is a window without any colour. The walls too may be colourless. The building may be colourless. When it rains steadily outside, will Rahel come and stand near her colourless window?

Yohannan did not see Ephraim return. He had given the umbrella to Sara and carried his own big umbrella with the curved cane handle. He thought Yohannan might have gone uphill and nearly passed without noticing him. But he was amazed to see Yohannan after all, standing like a shadow, wet and close to the tree.

'Are you still standing here, wet and shivering in the rain? Didn't I tell you to go uphill?' His voice was a little hard. Tilting his umbrella a little toward Yohannan, he said, 'Come, let us go.'

'No.' Yohannan muttered.

'What?' he asked eagerly stretching out his neck.

'I'm not coming.'

'You will catch cold and die if you stand here, I warn you.'

'Ephraim*chettan*, please go away.'

'Stay here, if you are so headstrong. The rain will become heavier.'

The rain was growing steadily. Ephraim went his way, cursing Yohannan in his mind. Once or twice, he turned and looked down. Yohannan was still standing at the foot of the tree. It supplied Ephraim with some special news to share with the Vicar.

The Vicar had not gone indoors. Instead, he stood helplessly watching the rain. Ephraim closed his umbrella and approached the Vicar, aggrieved to have stirred out in such a heavy rain.

'Returned so soon?'

Ephraim was amazed by this question. 'I gave the umbrella and I returned.'

When he was about to tell him how hard it was to persuade Sara to take the umbrella, the Vicar said, 'You should have accompanied her to the house.'

'It did not occur to me.'

'It is raining and almost dark.'

Ephraim began to feel a little guilty. He felt he should not have sent her alone in the thickening darkness and rain. O, but no. It is not that dark. It seems dark because of the rain. Sara must be home by now. Besides, she was walking very fast.

'By the by, I forgot. That boy, Yohannan, is standing drenched in rain, by the roadside, down below.'

'You mean our Thoma's son?'

'Yes. I told him to come to you and went after Sara to give her the umbrella. But when I returned, he was still standing there. He is standing under the tree.'

'Didn't you ask him here?'

'I did. But he seemed not to hear. I warned him that he would catch a fever if he got wet in the rain and that it is going to rain more heavily. But he won't budge.'

'I suppose, I will go and look.'

'No, Father,' Ephraim was in a panic when the Vicar picked up the umbrella. 'No, you shouldn't go. It is torrential rain. I'll go and look once again.'

'O, don't mind it. In this heavy rain, he...' The Vicar took Ephraim's umbrella and went out. Ephraim stood there, worried.

But when the Vicar went down and looked, Yohannan was nowhere to be found. He went close to the dripping tree. He cast his eyes all around and as far as he could see. Yohannan was already gone.

When Katrina asked, 'What have you decided?' Sara replied, 'I don't think leaving this place will put an end to my sorrow.'

Katrina said, 'There is no sorrow like your sorrow.'

With a pained smile, Sara said to herself, 'Yes, there is no sorrow like mine.'

'Sara, you cannot live here alone. Come with us. Let us sell this property. Of course, buyers will reduce the price, when we sell it suddenly. Leave it to Henry's father. He will manage it without great loss. Don't worry about it. With what we get, we will purchase land in our parish in your name. There, the land is more fertile. This land here has no fertility. Look at the black pepper and rubber. This land is not good. And a dead house too. How can you live here?'

Katrina went on talking. That Sara's life with Skaria was unfortunate…and that there was nothing to regret in his death, though it was premature…

'Sara, do you know how many nights I was sleepless thinking of you…sitting alone beside a dying man. I feel frightened, when I think of it.'

Katrina's children—Henry and Jiji*mol*—ran along the road toward the goats. The goats raised their heads and looked at the children.

'When I was a child, I was truly jealous of you. I wept, thinking I was not as beautiful as you, despite being born to the same parents. When you slept at night, I used to touch your cheeks and hair. You have become only more beautiful with the years. O, I feel like smiling. No, I will never smile, when you are living in sorrow. But, tell me, what have you decided? Won't you change your mind? Lord, this is sheer stubbornness. The same obstinacy you showed in your marriage. Father objected to this connection, but you insisted. Listen to me. Don't misunderstand me. I am not finding fault…'

Was it not because the marriage was against God's will, that Sara could not bear children to Skaria, wondered Katrina.

Then Sara remembered Skaria. You never gave me children. The reason may be that God had shut my womb. But we were given a three-year-old calf, a three-year-old goat, a three-year-old ram, a turtledove, and a nestling pigeon—

'But the Lord will hear your cry. You will get a good mate again. You will bear children. You will have a life. Girl, it can't be otherwise. I swear to you. He will remember all your offerings. All your desires will be fulfilled.'

A cool wind blew, bringing consolation. Katrina*chechi* and her children are going back. The children stand waving their hands. Katrina*chechi* is looking back again and again. She is not happy to leave, seeing me alone here. She has entrusted me to the care of our neighbours, Sosamma*chedathi*, Brigithamma, and Philipos*chettan*. *Chechi* has to go. Unless she goes, everything at home will be thrown into disorder. The older children are going to school. They have to be fed, dressed, and sent to school at the right time. Besides, there is the interrupted farm work. Henry's father has recently developed a severe stomach pain...

The woods sway in the wind. The wind is growing strong. *Chechi* and her children have disappeared beyond the trees. The sky has darkened. The earth is without its evening glow. The leaves are whirling. Dust is flying up. The windows slam shut.

I cannot stand here like this, I'd better go indoors, Sara thought.

Inside the room, Sara opened the windows and looked at the sky. She felt as if somebody was looking at her from the middle of the clouds. A shadow fell on her face. She stood for a long while, remembering something.

Then Sara shut the door and fastened the bolt. She removed her clothes one by one. She did it with order and neatness, like a ritual. In the dim light of the room, Sara's body shone uncovered. Bending her face, she looked at her breasts. She touched them. Alarmed, they yielded to her fingers.

Sosamma*chedathi* and Brigithamma came before dark.

'A rain is waiting, ready to fall.' Sosamma*chedathi* said.

That rain began to fall when they were spreading the reed mat to sleep on. It came rushing like ghosts and pressed against the house.

'I am scared,' Brigithamma said.

'Are you a babe in arms to be scared?' Sosamma*chedathi* laughed at her.

Brigithamma was the daughter of Sosamma*chedathi*'s son, Philipos. After school, she studied at a parallel college for some time. Now she was sitting idle at home. She had brought a book to read—a story book, it seemed. Lying prone on the mat, she scanned the pages in the light of the lamp. She held one end of her string of white stones in her mouth.

Looking at Sara, Sosamma*chedathi* said, 'You are very young. You should find another partner soon. Don't be cross with me. It has always been my nature to be blunt.'

Brigithamma tried hard to stifle her smile. Sosamma*chedathi* glared at her. 'Skaria was a good fellow. He was not crooked like others. Occasionally he used to drink a little. What of that? At times, men should drink a little. Otherwise, they have nothing to do. But excessive drinking is trouble. My Philipos's father—his name was Vareeth—never drank at the pub. Instead, he would bring the bottle home. He would hand it over to me and say, 'Sosamma, pour it as you please.' He was never obstinate. He would drink what I gave him and go to sleep. To tell you the truth, without that drink, he was just a dry branch. There was no stirring. Just… O, this damn clever girl… How quick she grasps things like this! If only she had been that clever at school. Ugh, what was I saying? Yes, now I remember, Philipos's father…'

A monsoon holy mass: Beware that you are not led away with the error of the wicked and fall from your steadfastness. But grow in the grace and knowledge of our Lord and Saviour, Jesus Christ. To him may be glory both now and forever. Amen.

Sara sorrowed. I am left behind. Always there is wind and storm. In the wind, the trees begin to break and fall. When the rain clears, Philipos*chettan*'s pigs wander in the compound.

Five or six of them occupy the compound, as if they owned it. They don't need words of courtesy and civility. They too are alive. Are they so content with life that they have nothing to feel sorrow for?

Perhaps one day, after making a circuit of the hillocks, they will come to the doorstep and begin to exchange pleasantries. Wagging their little tails, they may speak about life and death.

O, nothing to fear. Sara consoled herself: the pigs will never speak—at least to humans. They may be speaking to each other in the sty. What news? asks one pig. The woman next door is sorrowing, replies another pig. Her husband is dead and gone. She won't move away. Her sister tried to persuade her. But she won't leave this place. The old woman of this house and her son's daughter sleep there at night for company. Either the old woman or the girl will be there to keep her company at night. But for how long? The parishioners have started wondering what she is doing. Some say, she has a screw loose.

When Sara raised her head, she saw someone coming through the rain. He seemed quite unaware of the rain. While she was wondering who it was, he came to the courtyard. He hesitated for a while and then stepped into the veranda. Sara was stunned. He hung his head. Rainwater dripped from his hair onto his face, from his face onto his shirt, and from the shirt onto the floor. Poor boy! He is drenched from head to toe, thought Sara. She took a towel and held it out to him. He hesitated for a while, but she insisted. As he was wiping himself dry, Sara went in. A little while later, she returned with a cup of steaming coffee. He blew on it to cool it and drank.

'My name is Yohannan,' he said. 'A man called Thoma is my father and the late Theresa was my mother. Paolo, who hanged himself to death in fear of disgrace, is my grandfather. Annie, who eloped with the Assistant Vicar and left the parish, is my sister.'

Peter saw Yohannan coming out of Sara's house. He asked Yohannan where he had been. Yohannan said he had been to Sara's house. It surprised Peter.

He went straight to Sara's courtyard and called out to ask if anybody was there.

Sara was in her room. The rain was over and gone.

When she came out, Peter said, 'I was passing this way and just stopped by.'

On the hillsides after the rain, the blades of grass were heavy with raindrops. Yohannan walked with a feeling of alienation.

'I know all the parishioners feel sad about Sara. I go to most of the houses every day. The Vicar says, Sara is a riddle. He must have felt like that.'

Yohannan looked at the river. It flowed mud-red. It seemed a whole red hill was dissolved in the river. A tree trunk drifted in the current. If he wanted, he could go swimming and capture it. No need, Yohannan decided.

'Ng-ha, Sosamma*chedathi* has come. While passing this way, I thought I must just step in as a courtesy. Ha-ha, what *Chedathi* said is true. I am one who carries all information. I make it known to the persons concerned, regardless of time or context. When I see some letters, I know it is dangerous to deliver them now. But there is no way I can hold them back. I must deliver them to the addressees. It's the law, isn't it? I deliver the letter, and people, who have been laughing in their houses, start crying before I am out of the compound. Yes, everything is God's will. O, you shouldn't have taken the trouble to make this coffee. If I drink coffee from every house I visit, my belly will become as vast as the lake Vembanad. Ha-ha...no, that won't do. *Chedathi* also should join. Coffee is good in old age. But *Chedathi* looks only thirty...or at most, thirty-five...Ha-ha...Let me leave. When I sit to chat, I don't realize how much time goes by. I have more letters to deliver. I never saw any of the goddamn children in the shops. I wish I could finish all this, before it rains. O, isn't that a cat? Let me take it. O, is it so? Then, no, I won't take it. This house does need a cat.'

Goddamn it! It was a meaty cat. But the old woman Sosamma interfered. May the devil take her!

I know him. He is not an honest man. Come to enquire about Sara's welfare! Liar! He never took the trouble of coming this way when Skaria was alive.

Ha! Isn't life more than food and the body more than clothing? Looking at the darkness, Yohannan lay in his room. The darkness was thickening. Yohannan was naked. He lay with his eyes open.

He felt frightened when he thought of having reached Sara's house, while walking aimlessly in the pouring rain. At the same time, he felt great self-contempt. There was no need to go there. But, while walking, he had never thought of it at all. He had walked slowly and indifferently.

It was raining. On the road, lay fallen leaves and flowers. Not leaves and flowers, but the corpses of dead leaves and flowers. They lay in the heartless rain, beneath the immense sky.

The trees shivered with cold. The rain fell on the naked rocks. The hill hid in the rain. The tips of the bamboo shed tears. Water flowed. Water flowed over my head. The wind blew.

By then, my heart was drawn so very close to the heart of the earth. They brushed each other. I was soaking wet. I was thirsty. Now I feel fine. Yes. The coffee is very good. It is hot and bitter. Mother used to make such coffee. Later, Annie and I tried several times in vain to make it. What really matters is not the ingredients—coffee, jaggery, and black pepper—but the hands and the mind that go into its making. I have arrived at such a conclusion. Yes, I feel better. My body has stopped shivering. I don't feel cold anymore.

I am naked, I tell myself. I like to lie like this in the dark. My body is better than clothing. I run my fingers over my cheeks and through my hair. I feel my ears and lips touching them. My body is as fragrant as bread. It begins to rejoice like a caged bird freed from captivity. It flies as far as it can go, until its wings become tired.

Father is in the next room. It is a different world. He is there, asleep.

I sanctify me for myself…

In the next room, Father is sleeping. The wall stands between the rooms. The wall is strong. It is impossible to distinguish the door in darkness. The door is lost in the darkness.

I am alone here. I rest my face in my cupped fingers. O, I have been wandering among the flowers in some valley until now. My fingers speak of a garden. My eyelids begin to droop…

Sara woke up early in the morning. She did not know what time it was. She lay awake listening to the sounds from the hills.

Brigithamma was saying something in her sleep. She seemed to be speaking to someone, maybe to the hero of the novel she was reading last night.

When she sleeps, Brigithamma keeps her mouth open. She looks as if she's smiling. It is her habit from infancy.

When Brigithamma pulled the blanket over her and turned on her side, Sara rose and opened the door. It was slightly cold outside. Sara opened the door. Brigithamma lay wrapped in her blanket. Opening the door, Sara went out.

Sara had bathed and was ready by the time Brigithamma woke up.

'*Chechi*, have you bathed already when it is so early and icy cold?' she asked.

She crouched in her blanket.

'Is it so cold?' asked Sara.

'Look, it is misty everywhere.' The valley lay asleep under a white blanket.

'I feel very cold, let me light the fire.' Brigithamma rose to her feet. Sara smiled.

As the fire blazed in the hearth, Brigithamma stretched her hands toward it and felt the heat.

Sara also sat beside the hearth. Looking her in the face, Brigithamma asked, '*Chechi*, how long will you live alone?'

'I don't know.' Sara said.

'Somebody will marry you soon, *Chechi*.'

Brigithamma smiled. When she smiled her face became small.

Suddenly the fire hissed and crackled. Brigithamma asked Sara what those sounds meant. Sara did not know. Then Brigithamma said, 'This *chechi* does not know anything.' Sara admitted it with a thin smile. The fire blazed on. When Sara was about to make coffee, Brigithamma held her hand out and said, 'No, I'll make the coffee.' Sara yielded to her.

Brigithamma came again at noon. She soon made the purpose of her visit clear, beginning with a comment on her grandmother. 'That woman cannot tolerate novels and stories.' She wanted to finish the novel she had read half way. Her mind was throbbing to know what happened, in the face of bitter opposition, to the steadfast love between Thanka*chen*, who was poor, and Molly, the heiress.

'*Chechi*, let me sit here somewhere and finish reading the novel,' Brigithamma pleaded.

She sat aside in a corner. In a few moments, she closed the book in acute agitation, completely lost in the world of Thanka*chen* and Molly. She heaved a long sigh. Then, helplessly, she returned to the novel thinking, 'What will be will be.'

Sara did her chores or simply sat idle, looking at the hills. In the afternoon, she was alone again. Signs of approaching rain became visible outside. It came rushing from the west and Sara stood amazed. When the rain fell into her courtyard, Sara said, 'Here I am.'

She came out and stood in the courtyard. The rain ran toward Sara. Crying to herself, Sara stood in the rain.

Holding the mirror, Yohannan walked to the veranda. Nothing was visible beyond the rain falling in the courtyard.

Sitting on the bench, Yohannan looked at the rain.

It may be raining like this in Rahel's convent and Joshi's seminary. But they won't be alone there like this boy called

Yohannan. They will have many friends. When Joshi raises his face from the word of God in the Bible, he will see friends in sacred vestments.

And Rahel will see girls standing in deep meditation, forgetting themselves. It may be raining outside.

Yohannan's heart darkened. Heavy shadows fell on his eyes. But he found a way to comfort himself. Taking a beedi from the packet his father had left on the table, he put it to his lips. He breathed in and felt the taste of tobacco on his tongue and in his throat. Good. He took the box of matches. He was inexperienced and three match sticks blew out in the rainy wind. 'O, this has to be done with great caution,' Yohannan said to himself.

His fourth attempt succeeded. Smoke came out. He liked it.

He held the mirror up. He looked at his image in the mirror. He saw his broad forehead, the hair falling over it, large eyes, downy hairs, his pale lips and the tip of his tongue.

He smiled lightly. He opened his mouth as wide as possible. He put his tongue out. He ran his finger over his lower lip. He felt love for himself.

Brigithamma was reading the column 'Ask Your Doctor' in the weekly and laughed.

She started reading it out loud.

'I am seventeen years old. I have good health and beauty. Menstruation is normal. But, of late—'

Suddenly she lowered her voice, sensing that a sensitive bit was coming up. Sara heard: 'Two years and three months have passed after our marriage. We have no children. Husband's sem…sem…sem…'

Sara looked away from Brigithamma and out at the valley. It was blowing and raining. Someone was walking through the rain. There was stifled thunder.

The rain climbed on to the veranda in the wind. Brigithamma said, 'O, it is raining here,' and went into the room.

Sara stayed on the veranda.

When there was loud thunder, Brigithamma called, '*Chechi*, come inside! Don't sit there.'

Sara did not hear it at all. Her ears were deafened by the sound of the rain. She was startled when Brigithamma came and touched her on the shoulder. When she asked her what the matter was, Sara said, 'It is nothing,' and followed her.

Sara sat leaning on the wall at one end of the coir bed. She turned the pages of the weekly listlessly. Her eyes were not registering either the words or the pictures in it. Though she tried, she could not concentrate on anything. She set the weekly aside, as it did not serve any purpose. Brigithamma watched her.

'*Chechi*, please say something. Keeping mum like this…' said Brigithamma.

Sara smiled wanly. 'It is nothing, girl,'

Brigithamma thought seriously for a moment.

'Let me tell you something. *Chechi*, don't be cross with me.'

'Tell me.' Sara looked eagerly at her face.

Brigithamma again hesitated.

'What?'

'No, I'm not saying it. *Chechi* won't like it.'

Sara drew near. She put her hand on her shoulder. Looking into Sara's eyes, Brigithamma whispered, '*Chechi*, you should go away anywhere from here. I fear for your safety.'

Getting no answer, Brigithamma took Sara's face in her cupped hands and said again, 'Go away anywhere.' She was quite overcome by her feelings.

It was then that Sosamma*chedathi* called Brigithamma loudly from outside. Though Sosamma*chedathi*'s harsh voice entered the room, Brigithamma did not hear it.

Sara did hear it.

'She is calling you. Go and see why she is calling,' Sara said.

'*Chechi*, go away anywhere,' said Brigithamma.

'She is calling you. Go and see why she is calling,' Sara said again.

Brigithamma left with a heavy heart. Sara was alone. But she felt no grief. Sara rose to her feet and looked at her face in the mirror hanging on a nail near the window. The mirror was misted over. The mirror was in mourning. So, the mirror did not receive Sara as usual. She wiped it clean. The mirror's sorrow ended.

Then Sara fell on the bed and imagined a journey. 'Go away anywhere,' said Brigithamma. Yes, I must go anywhere… anywhere… Here, I have started. I am walking out into the rain, taking off my clothes one by one. I am walking naked through the valley. It is raining. My body is soaking wet in the rain. I am walking through the woods. I am walking past the tangled roots and vines. Leaving the dark way behind, I am entering the way where light dwells. I am wandering among the clumps of grass. Climbing the hill, I arrive in the church courtyard. 'Father, Father—' I call. He comes in his long robe and with eyes full of compassion. 'I have come to see you, only to see you. I thought I ought to see you.' He takes my hands: 'Come.' We stand in front of the altar. 'Feel comforted, daughter,' says Father with kindness. I feel stifled. I become restless. 'Why do you mortify yourself like this, daughter? How completely changed you are after Skaria died!' He runs his fingers through my hair. I can hear the echoing sound of rainwater dripping from my hair. My eyes fly off somewhere. 'How completely changed you are!' I kneel at his feet: 'Father, my life is filled with bitterness. There is nothing but weeping and sorrow. The joy of my heart has ceased. My dance is turned into mourning. Water flows over my head. I am lost.' Standing for a while thoughtfully, Father bends and caressing my wet hair says: 'Why don't you smile?' I lift my face pitiably. 'Can you tell me a parable on the mercy of God?'

Yohannan felt somebody calling him. Lifting his slightly red-rimmed eyes, he looked around. But he did not see anyone. He rose to his feet and looked outside. He thought it was his imagination and sat down again. Then he heard an injunction: 'You shall not uncover the nakedness of your father's wife. You shall not uncover the nakedness of your father.' Yohannan was frightened. Where are the words coming from? Who? Terrified, he ran into his room. The room was in darkness and he became more terrified. He rushed back to the veranda. He looked around, panting. There was nobody there. He sat on the bench and sighed. The rain had almost subsided. Only a thin drizzle and a moist wind remained.

Once again he held the mirror to his face. Then he heard the echo: 'You shall not uncover the nakedness of your father. It is abomination.'

Dropping the mirror on the floor, he ran away. Afraid that someone was chasing him, he turned and looked back.

The road was deserted. He went down straight into the woods. He hurried along the river bank. As he walked, he thought of the thing that had frightened him. That voice... he felt it echoing again in his ears. Lord! Was it not the voice of Grandfather? He was bewildered. Yes. It is his voice, sure. He said, do not uncover your father's nakedness and that it is abomination. Yes, yes, it is him, no doubt. When Father quarreled with him on account of Rahel...now everything becomes clear. It was what grandfather said to his son. I happened to overhear it accidently. Perhaps Grandfather said this on earlier occasions too. Or he is giving me a warning. Yohannan was perplexed.

But there was no a ghost on the road; not even a pale ghost.

The sky was white after the rain. The face of the sky was as solemn as a priest officiating the last rites. Yes, the earth is sinful. On earth are lament, adultery, and theft. Men look for a chance to cheat one another. However... However, the sky cannot abandon the earth. It cannot shower one more curse on the damned earth in its ruinous course and run away. The sky cannot deviate from its appointed place, but can only remain sympathetic, remembering old prayers and sacrifices. Under this sky, sins and sinners will keep increasing. After all, who is a sinner? What is sin?

Suppose somebody asked, the Vicar would say: You should not sin to yourself. You should not lie with a person of the same sex. You should not mate with an animal. Do not kill. Do not commit adultery. Do not steal. Do not bear false witness against your neighbour. You shall not covet your neighbour's house. You shall not covet your neighbour's wife, or male or female slave, or ox, or donkey, or anything that belongs to your neighbour. You shall not abuse any widow... You...You...

I saw. Here, a pale horse. The name of its rider was Death. Hell followed him. He was given authority over a quarter of the earth, to kill with sword, famine, and pestilence, and by the wild animals of the earth. Closing the *Book of Revelation*, Sara looked toward the treetops and the sky that appeared above them, like a huge wing of a bird. Sara felt grief.

Then Brigithamma was in the company of a boy. His name was Paul. Having found a secluded place in the middle of the rocks and thickets, they were trying to discover something. Paul's hands shivered visibly. His body flooded with heat and was covered in sweat. He swallowed back the lump in his throat. He touched Brigithamma's lip with his sweaty finger. That touch burnt his finger. His mind was filled with anxiety and fear. He said, 'I am scared.' Hearing this, Brigithamma found it hard to suppress her laughter. He again said, 'No, I am scared.' Smiling enigmatically, she removed her blouse. He looked around, feeling panic rising within him. In his heart, he prayed to the Holy Spirit. Leaping to his feet, he said, 'I'm going.' He ran without listening to what she had to say.

Brigithamma was stunned. She was about to call him, but decided not to. She sat there thinking. She felt sorry for having attempted such an adventure with a younger boy. How trivial a character that boy is! A coward! Anyway, it is a shame. She sat biting her finger. Her eyes were moist. Then the boy returned. Standing at a distance, holding a drooping branch, he said, 'I won't tell anyone. Don't be afraid.'

Having made that promise, he ran away.

His promise did not have the desired result. It only made Brigithamma more helpless. She slowly put on her clothes. Smoothing her hair with her hands, she came out of the hide-out. She became her old self. She moved like a sacral scent.

When she came near Sara's house, she thought of dropping in.

The air was filled with the stink of pigs. Pigs wandered across the hillsides in search of feed. They trotted about, wagging their little tails and grunting lightheartedly, without the burden of collective memories or pride of birth or genealogies.

When they saw Brigithamma coming, they raised their faces and grunted.

Unmindful of the pigs and raising her skirt a little, she ran lightly toward the house.

Scarcely had she reached the courtyard, when she stopped abruptly.

Sara was not alone; Yohannan also was there. They were talking and laughing.

Brigithamma hesitated. When she quite unexpectedly saw another boy, she had a feeling of nausea thinking of her shameful experience a little while ago. For the first time, she became conscious of having a secret to keep. Her face sagged.

'Come, why have you stopped there?' asked Sara.

'Nothing,' Brigithamma walked toward the house, embarrassed. She could not look at Yohannan.

'Where have you been?'

'Just out.'

'*Chedathi* has been here looking for you.'

'Ng-he…?'

A lightning shock passed through Brigithamma's mind.

'I've just been to a friend's house. I forgot to tell them at home.'

'*Chedathi* said you told them you were coming here.'

'I'm going.' She turned and started walking.

'Stop, do you know Yohannan?' Sara asked.

Brigithamma turned once again toward them. She looked first at Sara, and then at Yohannan. He sat with his head bowed, so Brigithamma found it easy to look at him.

She knew Yohannan, by way of Annie. She knew about his grandfather hanging himself to death and Annie running away with the Assistant Vicar. In this parish, there is only one house, where a father and son live with no one else to care for them.

Yes, Brigithamma knew Yohannan. But she wondered what brought him there. Maybe he casually dropped in, while passing this way. But she could not recall ever seeing him come this way before. His slightly dark face, doubtless, has a special charm. What! His curly hair, lips, and long neck—that boy touched my lip with his finger...the way he sat—the boy said he was scared. Poor boy! He was really scared. What if he tells people? He has given me his word. Yes, but can I trust him? Will he confess it to the priest? Lord! Brigithamma withdrew her eyes, as Yohannan raised his face.

'*Chechi*, I'm going. I'll come a little later.'

Yohannan's eyes followed Brigithamma, who hurried away without looking back. Making sure she was gone, he turned again to Sara. He had left his house feeling that somebody had called him. He ended up here. The widow sat on the veranda, reading the Bible. He looked at Sara carefully. What is between Sara and me, he wondered.

'I have no one,' he said.

When she heard his words, she smiled into his eyes. He had said this a little while ago.

'I had seen Skaria*chettan* being taken to the hospital.'

'He died.' After a while, she added, 'It is good that he died.'

Yohannan looked at Sara amazed.

'Yakob*chettan*, who died, used to fault God.'

'Why?'

'He used to fault God for making you marry Skaria*chettan*.'

'O,' Sara sighed. 'He was a nuisance.'

'Who do you mean? Yakob*chettan* was not a nuisance in the general sense. Nobody understood him.'

Sara did not agree with him. In her heart, Yakob was a dark shadow. How could she forget those days when he constantly followed her?

'I was the last to see him alive, before he died on the river bank. He gave me some arrack he had made from cashew juice.'

'Yohannan, do you drink arrack?'

'I've never had it again.'

'Didn't your father know?'

'It seems not. It doesn't matter, even if he knows.'

He smiled, and so did Sara. It was then that Brigithamma had arrived.

When she was gone, Yohannan returned to Sara.

To Sara…To Sara…

Who else in the parish other than Sara can he open his heart to? he thought. It does not require an explanation. It is a mystery that is not unraveled. There are so many things like this in this world.

In Yohannan's mind, Sara stood among those who have graced the world with their beauty and humility, and who have refused to fault God for their personal tragedies. (How small a number it is!) The love and sympathy Yakob had felt for Sara had touched Yohannan from the very beginning. It had been disturbing him as a riddle. Skaria's death certainly made him more concerned about Sara. (Probably Sara said it was good that he died in the sense that God had ended his sufferings and carried off his soul.) Yakob's death had an equal importance. If Yakob had been alive when Skaria died, Yohannan would not have imagined Sara as a dove descending upon his soul. He had great regard for Yakob's arguments. His death had shaken Yohannan badly. It also had an inexplicable mystery about it. As if God's anger had suddenly fallen.

Sara's remark about Yakob was unfair, he felt. Nobody in the parish remembered him. His story ended with his death. Will his soul attain rest? Or will it wander ever restlessly over this parish witnessing joy and sorrow?

'I—' Yohannan began hesitatingly and sadly. 'I came here by chance, as I have nowhere else to go. The place I go to, occasionally, is the cemetery. My mother is there. Sometimes I sit near her and cry. Yesterday, too, Annie*chechi* called me to town. But I will never go. I will not go anywhere. It seems you have also decided not to leave. I know you have relatives in another parish and that they urge you to leave this place. I have also heard parishioners wonder about why you stay here. They all wonder how Sara will live here alone. They sneak around and watch you. I know you…'

In one breath, Yohannan bent forward, took Sara's right hand and fervently kissed it. Then he did not stay a moment. Sara was about to say something, but he did not look back.

Instantly, Sara forgot what she was about to say. As he walked away in distress, she sat damned like a pillar of salt. She felt as if she was choking.

Her right hand wandered to her Bible. Sweat broke out on her forehead. Lord! When she thought of it, her heart burned.

Leaping to her feet, Sara went into the room to find darkness. Yes, she managed to escape the light, but her confusion did not leave her. Rather, it only increased. Her body became covered in sweat. She wished Brigithamma or Sosamma*chedathi* were there. She even considered going to see Sosamma*chedathi*.

Sara seldom visited other houses. Probably because of her situation and state of mind, even her neighbours never encouraged her to visit. Though they attempted to make friends in the early days, she always turned down their invitations. When Anna, a simple-minded woman living east of Sara's house, complained of Sara's haughty nature, Sosamma*chedathi* had defended Sara, saying that a young widow like Sara would take a fairly long time to forget her sorrow and recover her mental health. When she heard this from Sosamma*chedathi* herself, Sara felt boundless gratitude. There was something to be said for talkativeness.

Sara thought of meeting Sosamma*chedathi* and confessing everything to her. She never thought of the consequences. She hastily washed her face and mouth. When she came to the courtyard, smoothing her disheveled hair with her wet hands, she saw the nuns at a distance.

Sister Mithria and Sister Marianos were out on an evening walk. They are in the habit of walking most days in one or the other direction of the parish. Sometimes, they wander aimlessly on the hillsides or walk as far as the forest. As it is usually dark in the forest by the time they get there, they turn away from the narrow path and walk back. They plan to explore all around the forest one day, in the company of an able guide.

Sara stood alarmed, when she saw Sister Mithria and Sister Marianos coming. They were among the last visitors Sara might have expected at that time.

Sara stood watching their silent tread.

When they came near, smiling with sympathy, Sara recovered herself. She reverently invited them to come into the veranda and sit.

Sister Mithria said, 'We have no time to sit. It is very late. And it may rain. We will come at our leisure one day. We thought to just see you and go.'

Sara bowed her head. Placing her hand on Sara's shoulder, 'Sister Marianos, don't be upset. God belongs to Sara too.'

With a few words, they took her painful heart in their hands, swaying, caressing, and kissing it. They left, restoring serenity to her heart. She felt that all her wounds were healed.

Feeling consoled, Sara heaved a sigh of relief. Instead of visiting Sosamma*chedathi*, she started to prepare a simple supper.

Dusk approached. A wind blew, announcing the rain on a distant hill. The parish wished wholeheartedly for a night absolutely full of goodness.

Thoma was viewing the saint's idol displayed for public obeisance. It shook him. He lay on his back looking at thick darkness. His heart became distressed thinking of the grace God showered not only on those who led a pious life—regularly taking the sacraments, reading the Bible daily, and doing good to their neighbours—but also on morose people like him.

A green pasture, a flock of sheep, a clear stream... Thoma felt an irrepressible desire to reveal to someone what he saw in his sleep and his ensuing state of mind. He did not have the patience to wait until morning. What if he forgot everything meanwhile?

He leaped to his feet, opened the door and called Yohannan.

Yohannan was sleeping, as still as a dead leaf. When Thoma hopefully called him twice or thrice, Yohannan woke up. He was dismayed. Father was lighting the lamp. On his face was a bright, tender smile. Seeing it, his dismay was all the more heightened. He wondered what special thing had happened to wake him up in the middle of the night. His eyes were heavy with sleep.

After lighting the lamp, Thoma lighted a beedi. Yohannan pulled away his blanket and sat up. He looked at his father with drooping eyes.

'It is nothing. I wanted to tell you something.' Thoma puffed out the smoke, slightly embarrassed.

Yohannan did not ask him what the matter was. Thoma sat completely absorbed in a feeling of piety and bliss, thinking of the idol he saw in his vision.

'I did not know what the occasion was. There were illuminations, fireworks, and the crowd. No, I cannot say what the event was. And there was the idol of the saint.'

Yohannan turned his face away in displeasure, convinced that his father, who was senselessly drunk, was simply disturbing him.

Thoma continued, 'I was thinking…what God had kept in store for me too was a good dream. It is always like that. You go to sleep. I am snuffing out the lamp.'

Saying this much, he put out the lamp and went out as if deeply ashamed of his actions. He did not forget to close the door behind him.

He should not have woken Yohannan. Thoma felt sorry. It was a long time since he had spoken freely to his son. Yohannan must have been stumped. O, never mind. Throwing away the beedi stub, he strolled aimlessly in the courtyard. He lit another beedi and looked up at the sky. Stars spread all over the sky. The night was cold.

Yohannan somehow passed a week without going out anywhere. When it became intolerable, he went out one afternoon.

Thoma was utterly perplexed by Yohannan's behaviour in the last week. Afraid to face him in daylight, he set off early in the morning. When he returned in the evening, Yohannan was sitting against the pigsty. When Thoma asked him why he was sitting there, he got up and went indoors without saying anything. It was Thoma who prepared supper that day. When called to supper, Yohannan came readily, like an automaton. His behaviour appeared reproachable to Thoma. Though Thoma watched him through the meal, Yohannan did not know it. His attitude was more or less the same in all the days that followed. When Thoma asked him what was wrong with him, and whether he was sick, he replied listlessly that he was all right. Thoma made up his mind to speak to the Vicar about Yohannan.

When Yohannan went out that afternoon, Thoma happened to be home. After his mid-day meal, lying on the bed on the veranda, he smoked a beedi. He tried to remember things without any sequence or orderliness. Theresa also came into his mind. As he was about to doze off, wishing that her soul rest in peace, Yohannan went out. He did not even look in the direction of his father. Thoma asked where he was going. He walked away without replying. Later, postman Peter told Thoma that it was to Sara's house Yohannan had gone. Thoma was curious to know what business Yohannan had at Sara's house.

Thoma and Peter were on their way to the church. Thoma wanted to meet the Vicar and talk to him. On the road he met Peter, who was going to deliver the Vicar's letters, and happened to mention Yohannan to him. Thoma said he was going to speak to the Vicar about his son, who had of late become quite listless and uninterested in anything. Peter gaped at him when he heard this.

'I saw him a little while ago, near that Sara's house,' said Peter. 'Yes, I saw him exactly there. I don't know what business he has there. However, I saw him there three or four times.'

'Sara who…?

'Skaria's widow…'

Peter crossed himself in memory of Skaria.

Thoma became worried. 'Why should he go there?'

'He may know that. He is not a baby. Isn't he old enough to know a woman?'

Those words fell heavy as stones upon Thoma. Peter swore in the name of the Lord that he was not lying. Thoma did not hear it. The roads drag us to unknown destinations…

Ephraim came out and took the letters from Peter. The Father was writing something, Ephraim told Peter when he asked him where he was. Peter left and Ephraim ushered Thoma into the Father's room.

The Vicar sat writing in his armchair, a writing board placed across its arms.

When he saw Thoma, he received him with true happiness. 'Come, I have been waiting for a meeting with you,' said the Vicar, closing his pen.

'Am I interrupting your writing?' said Thoma with humility.

'O, no,' the Vicar shook his head. 'I was just finishing. Thoma*chen*, please sit down.'

Thoma sat near the wall, facing the Father's chair. When he was wondering how to start, Father said: 'I don't see you or your son here these days. I believe, he has never been here this monsoon.'

'I am here to ask you to call him and counsel him.'

'Good.' The Vicar said with genuine cheerfulness. 'I was about to call both of you. Anyway, at least I met you.'

Guilty and worried, Thoma sat with his head bent. 'I know, there was negligence on my part too, Father. But, please don't ask me the reason why.'

'Does it mean that I can expect you here on all occasions hereafter?'

'Yes.'

'I hope you are getting letters from your daughter?'

'She...sent some letters...but in truth, I have not read them. It seems she has stopped writing,' Thoma said with difficulty.

'Soon Annie will be the mother of a child.' The Vicar closed his eyes remembering her prayerfully. He smiled gently too.

Thoma was about to say something, but kept mum as Ephraim arrived with coffee. His heart faltered between Annie and Theresa. He felt grief. Then, in quite a tender voice, the Vicar said, 'I cannot hate them.'

'That is your personal view, isn't it, Father? The Holy Church has a different view,' Thoma said with a wounded heart.

Thoma did not explicitly say that his was the position of the Church. But it was obvious.

'I know your heart, Father. It is as large as the earth. Its largeness will include my daughter, who erred, as well as *Kochachen*, who sinned. But...when they make me a coffin, the largeness of this dishonour too has to be considered. In that coffin, this dishonour will not decay so easily...' Thoma faltered. He shook his head smiling in self-contempt.

The Vicar was confused as to how to console him. Finally, he said, 'Thoma*chen*, drink your coffee. It is specially made by Ephraim, with ginger and black pepper.'

Thoma obeyed. As the Vicar said, it was specially made, and good for a sore throat.

They were silent as they finished their coffee. The Vicar looked at the letters and words he had scribbled on the pad. Some of them had begun to fade.

'May I leave, Father?' Putting the tumbler near the window, Thoma got up to leave.

'You may go if you are in a hurry.' The Vicar placed the writing pad on the floor. He felt better when he came outdoors with Thoma. His body had become tired sitting idle in the room.

It was when Thoma started walking that the Vicar thought of Yohannan.

'Stop, you didn't tell me what was wrong with Yohannan.'

Putting his hands to his head, Thoma turned and said, 'O, I forgot. I forgot what I came for. You should call him and counsel him. If I try to advise him, he won't listen.'

'It's only the two of you at home, isn't it?'

'But, to be frank, there is no father-to-son closeness between us. I don't know how the problem started. I suppose it may be my fault. He is an introvert like Theresa. After she died, it was my father who brought him up. He ended in a shameful manner. And Annie abandoned us. I failed to give him the love of a father. Yes, it is my fault.'

'Isn't he writing the exam?'

'He says no.'

'Why?'

Thoma shrugged his shoulders.

'He was clever in studies, wasn't he?'

'Later everything changed.'

'You should have cared.'

'I told you, it is my fault. Now he has grown enough to make his own decisions.'

'Send him to me. Let me try. I will speak to him tomorrow.'

'Besides—'

The Vicar felt Thoma had something else to say and that he was a bit doubtful about saying it.

'What is the matter? Tell me.'

'I don't know, but Peter told me…'

'You mean postman Peter?'

'Yes.'

'What did he say?'

'When I heard it, I found it difficult to believe. Perhaps there is nothing of concern.'

'Thoma*chen* didn't tell me what the matter was.'

'How shall I tell you? Peter said that Yohannan was a frequent visitor at the late Skaria's house, where that woman... Skaria's widow is living all by herself, alone.'

'You mean Sara?'

'Yes.'

That accusation stunned the Vicar's senses. He stood stupefied looking at Thoma's face. His cyeballs became smaller and smaller and disappeared. His arms were lifted to his chest.

Bewildered, Thoma called him twice.

The Vicar nodded his head. It was Thoma's permission to leave.

Thoma hurried away.

Thoma felt what he said was a mistake and was disgraceful to God. He should not have relied on Peter's words and brought so serious an allegation before the priest. He should not have caused distress to his mind.

Terribly worried, Thoma looked back. The Vicar had not moved. Thoma's lips trembled as if bitten by a viper. He hurried away down the hill.

Sometime after Thoma had left, Yohannan came that way.

He was coming from Sara's house. Thinking of the cross on the hilltop, Yohannan walked toward the church. The Vicar was strolling in the church courtyard with bent head, his hands clasped behind him. So Yohannan could not see his face quite clearly.

He stopped and stood without making any noise. The priest turned and looked. He knew the presence of Yohannan. As soon as he realized that it was Yohannan, he eagerly walked toward him. When he came near, the Vicar only looked in his face with sympathy and did not ask him anything. The Vicar's eyes were filled with love and kindness. Yohannan saw his image deeply impressed in those eyes. Carried away by his feelings, he knelt before the priest, took his right hand, and awkwardly kissed it several times. Freeing his hand, the Vicar crossed himself and raised Yohannan to his feet.

'What happened to you, Yohannan? It has been ages since you last turned up. One day, I sent the sexton to enquire. The only thing he found out was that there was nobody in the house. Your face seems to have changed a lot. Thoma said you are no longer writing the exams. Is it true?'

'I cannot do it,' Yohannan said in a subdued voice.

'Will it suffice to say this? Don't let yourself regret it later. Or else, if you want to turn to farming for a living, there is nothing wrong with it. Then you must learn it from your father and help him with the work.'

Yohannan did not speak.

'I heard another thing, which even then I thought was baseless. Yet, I am asking you. Are you friendly with Skaria's widow, Sara?'

It was with great embarrassment that the Vicar asked him the question. He had resolved not to ask it, but he expected to hear that it was a false story.

When Yohannan heard the Vicar's unexpected question, he turned deathly pale. He felt the whole parish had been following him and watching his every movement. They were all conspiring against him.

He muttered, 'It is true.'

His hair fluttered in the wind.

'Did you lie with her?'

Yohannan was swept up in a cyclone. Like dust, he yielded to it. It carried him through the wagon roads, the trees and woods, the grasslands and the pastures. The sun was cool; the hillsides in the afternoon sun were yellow. It was dark wherever the sunlight did not fall. Yohannan felt the earth deserted. He saw no one anywhere. There were endless wastelands before him. He walked past the stones and the stumps of trees. His shadow moved through the lines of grass. As he walked with his own shadow, Yohannan realized that the earth was not deserted as he had supposed.

There was Peter on the road. Continuously twitching his cheeks in his peculiar manner, holding his letters in his hand, and dangling a huge umbrella from his back collar, Peter came from the opposite direction.

Peter said to Yohannan, 'Where are you going? Tell me.' There was no reply.

Peter was irritated. When he saw Yohannan go toward Sara's house, he asked him why he was acting like this.

Yohannan ignored him and walked on. Peter stood stunned. He walked away, muttering and scolding as he saw Yohannan disappear behind the coffee bushes and the lemon trees.

Yohannan reached the courtyard of Sara's house. Sara was not on the veranda. The door was closed.

His eyes were those of an unfledged bird that had been left helplessly alone in the nest.

Leaning on the bamboo prop, Yohannan stood amid the grunting of the pigs in the scorching sun, under the vast open sky. How lonely sits the city that once was full of people! How she, that was great among the nations, has become like a widow!

His heart was weeping.

The city whose gates are desolate! Zion who mourns, for no one comes to the festivals! She has no one to comfort her. Her heart is in distress. The carcasses of her dead priests lie about. Her pastures have been destroyed. Her palaces are ruined. Her ramparts have fallen. The fainting children in the streets are crying, 'Where is bread and wine?' It is a wound as vast as the sea.

Yohannan pressed his head on the bamboo prop, as if on a cross.

Mount Zion was desolate. He raised his eyes. A thick cloud blocked his prayer.

'Sara,' he called, entering her room.

The afternoon had lulled Sara to sleep. She lay on her right side, her hands folded under her head, on the coir bed near the wall beneath the window. Sleeping Sara looked like snow. Her lips seemed on the verge of a whimper.

Yohannan sat on the floor. Occasionally, he looked at Sara. Sara was clad in white.

He called her again, 'Sara.'

That call struck Sara, like a stone falling upon the tent. Sara woke up.

Sara was frightened, when she saw Yohannan sitting on the floor gazing at her. She leaped to her feet. Tying back her tousled hair, she moved to the corner. Her face was deathly pale. Yohannan faced her with a foolish smile. His eyes were dull.

'Sara,' he whispered.

'Go away,' she said.

'You are not willing to listen to me.'

He lowered his head unto the dust.

'I came looking for you. Do not abandon me.'

Sara was terribly frightened when he said this. Her spirit flapped its wings and cooed like a dove. It was in great distress.

He stretched out his hands and she came forward, crying and panting. At his arm's length, she too knelt like him. She received his right hand in her burning lips. Moving closer, she held his face in her hands, as if it were a dove. She sat thus looking into his wet and throbbing eyes—Sara was reflected in them. Then, in a sacred ritual, she drew her lips close to his forehead.

He rested his head on her sweaty shoulder.

She said, 'I will remove your soiled clothes. I will clothe you in the festive dress.'

Yohannan remembered all this, when he looked at the Vicar.

The Vicar waited eagerly for his reply. It was getting late.

'Yes,' said Yohannan.

When Sara came out of her house, a drop fell on her head from the clouds. She looked at the clouds pensively and then walked toward the nearby stream to bathe. She lay in the cold of the stream that ran through the darkened woods and the undergrowth. It calmed her. She heard the sound of rain from far away.

Yohannan remained standing in the river. Raindrops fell on his body and on the river. He stood looking at the bubbles, the falling raindrops, raised on the river. His body began to shiver in the cold.

The Vicar leaned on the pillar and looked at the rain drenching the valley. Ephraim warned him against standing there in the drizzle, but he did not move.

It was raining all over the valley.

Ephraim retreated into his room, offended at the Vicar for ignoring his benevolent advice. When he came out after some time to see what the Vicar was doing—

With a loud cry Ephraim ran out into the rain and caught the Vicar. When Ephraim asked him what he was doing, the Vicar did not reply. He was praying. His body was soaking wet.

Having examined himself and become convinced that he had behaved in a grossly indecent and childish way that evening, Thoma went to Isaac's pub and met him. Swallowing the four hundred milli of arrack Isaac accurately measured out, Thoma came home, feeling stupid. He sat down to wait for Yohannan.

Yohannan, on the other hand, stood naked in the river without knowing that his father was waiting for him. The rain fell on him.

It was very late. When Yohannan stepped into the veranda, along with the darkness and the rain, Thoma looked scornfully at him and turned his face away.

Considering his father's behaviour not unusual, Yohannan went to his room and changed his clothes. Then he tried to light a fire in the hearth.

Muttering to himself about running out of matches, Thoma came near the hearth to light a beedi that had gone out halfway. He had been smoking continuously since he came home. The fire blazed in the hearth. When Yohannan put a pot of neatly washed cassava on the flame and turned to go, Thoma said, 'Wait, I have a thing to tell you.'

Yohannan was bewildered. Thoma said, 'Come, sit here.'

Yohannan obeyed him. They both watched the fire.

'You live here with your heart elsewhere. You know this without my saying it. Of late, you've been behaving as if you do not belong here or this house has nothing to do with you. I don't know where this began. I admit there is something wrong with this house. Things were never right here. It is as if a curse had fallen on the house. But Theresa, your mother, fought it all her life. She was taken from us as a result of it. You are the one who remains. I am not going to marry again and produce children. Ng-ha, I can do that if I want. Several people have told me. But I did not pay heed to them.'

'For my sake.'

'Yes, for your sake,' Thoma replied a bit rudely. He took another beedi, throwing the spent one into the fire.

Yohannan poked the fire. What else was there in his father's mind, he wondered. He felt quite restless. Damn it.

'The Vicar said he wanted to meet you.'

'Why?'

Thoma controlled himself.

'You should meet him tomorrow morning. Then he will tell you why.'

'You must have babbled something to him,' Yohannan muttered.

Unfortunately, Thoma heard him over the roar of the fire. It incensed him. The restraint and moderation he had maintained evaporated. Those belittling words were quite unbearable. He leaped to his feet and raised his leg over the fire to kick the boy. Yohannan, frightened, scrambled up and accused his father of craziness and stupidity. Thoma became all the more angry. He shouted that Yohannan was committing adultery with an immoral woman called Sara. Yohannan reached him in one leap. Clutching the back of his father's neck with his left hand, he hit him hard on his face.

After all that agitation, they slept. They woke in the morning in shame and panic. Yohannan did not stir from where he lay on the floor, staring at the roof. He felt his eyes aching.

There was a mist outside. Thoma went out walking. He felt timid, wondering how to face Yohannan in daylight. When he heard me cry out his relation with an immoral woman called Sara, he became like a man possessed. Yes, he was possessed by the devil. His left hand caught me by the neck. With his right hand, he hit my face. He has been possessed by the devil. Letting me go, he ran into his room and slammed the door. It was the sound of the closing door that woke me from my stupor. He has been possessed by the devil. I banged on the door several times asking him to open it. He did not open it. He began to cry out loud. Was it out of fear or sorrow, I'm not sure. But he was wailing. I imagined him sitting on the floor close to the door, crying uncontrollably. I fell on my bed with a shiver. It was very late, when sleep came.

'I can't allow this to go on,' growled Thoma. He was resolved to take some action.

Yohannan was unable to make up his mind about anything. His face was apathetic and listless. He had felt his eyes aching when he woke up. Later, the pain was gone, but the memories remained. I wept a lot at night. Fear and helplessness had made my body tired. I ran into my room shutting the door behind me and fell fainting on the floor. My father repeatedly banged on the door. When he heard me cry, he might have left. I might have cried again for a long time. I fell asleep crying on the floor. Yes, I remember everything clearly. Self-contempt makes a shiver run through my body. I am cold and dusty from lying on the floor.

It is unbearable to remember. Let me lie here and go to sleep again. Maybe, I can spread the mat out and sleep on that. No. I am going to my dark secrecy, to my divine ritual, to my song of myself. I see bright candlelight. I see fresh new wine. I see my own body.

Despite a wounded heart, Thoma walked along with the weariness of a feverish man, searching for an effective way out. He became more distressed as he remembered one thing or the other. He approached Sara's house with the bewilderment and the dejection a sleepwalker feels when he suddenly becomes conscious and observes his surroundings. His perplexity increased when Sara came out, bathed, and clad in immaculate white.

'You know me, don't you?' he asked her, without thinking how to begin.

Sara's face flushed red.

'I did not have any relationship with Skaria worth mentioning. However, I knew him. I have come here too. Skaria was a good person. He was virtuous. But it is such people whom God calls too soon.' Thoma spoke with the fervour of an evangelist. Looking at his face, one would feel he was speaking to himself. And he was.

Thoma did not look at Sara. He climbed up and sat on the bench in the veranda without waiting to be asked. He lighted a beedi to relieve the steadily mounting tension.

Again he said, 'Samuel Sir's death too was a similar one. (May his soul rest in peace.) Before him died his innocent child. God's mercy did not fall on them. Yes, it should be put like that, even if it sounds like heresy. His wife is now in some convent or hospital. She spends her life consoling those, who are in tears and sorrow. God bring her good luck.'

When Thoma finished saying this, Sara retreated into her room panting and sighing. She was shivering from head to foot. Her legs faltering, scraping the wall, she slumped down to the floor. Then she cried, and Thoma heard her. He became timid and tried to pity her: 'Poor woman! She has already understood what I have been driving at. She is feeling sorry.'

But the next moment, when he thought of Yohannan, he felt vindictive and obstinate. There was nothing to regret about hurting her feelings. He decided to do what he had planned.

'You have understood what I said, haven't you?' He bent his head toward the door and his voice betrayed no tinge of softness.

'What did this fellow say?'

The question shook him. When he looked to see where the voice came from, he saw Sosamma*chedathi*. Thoma turned pale like a ghost.

Sosamma*chedathi* came toward him till she was inches away, glaring at him with irritation, then passed him, and went into the room.

'Sara, what is this? What happened?' She almost wept when she saw Sara's sorrowing face.

Thoma left. Hesitating and embarrassed, he looked about, worried that someone would see him in that condition. Time and again, he seemed to be in disgrace. Convinced that Thoma had done something to grieve Sara, Sosamma*chedathi* came out to scold him, but she found nobody there. It only enraged her more. She even walked some distance searching among the bushes, combing the branches to see whether the coward was hiding in there.

Yohannan spent the whole day by the sick bed of the Vicar and at the church. The Vicar was seriously ill with typhoid. Hearing reports of his illness, the anxious parishioners streamed to the parsonage. They all prayed wholeheartedly for his recovery. Though the Vicar was exhausted from the sudden attack of fever and his old age, he recognized Yohannan and softly pressed his hand. Ephraim took Yohannan out to tell him of the Vicar's rash adventure after Yohannan had left him the other evening.

'My child, the most painful sight I have seen in my life was the Vicar standing soaking wet in the rain. He neither stirred, nor moved, even though a whole monsoon season poured down on him. He stood there like an obstinate child. He was praying, lifting up his arms like a prophet in his majesty, unmindful of the rain and wind. His heart was afflicted by some agonizing pain, I'm certain. He might have prayed so fervently for someone else. I have no idea what happened. I cannot bear it…my child. What! Child, your eyes are filled with tears.'

For two weeks, the parish was plunged in fear and anxiety. On the day after the doctor's visit, the Father's fever suddenly shot up. He wandered between life and death with the remembrance of some past winter. Ephraim and the others were amazed that the priest in his delirium was always talking about winter. Later, when Ephraim reminded him of this, the Vicar only sat pensive and did not give any explanation.

The Vicar lay unconscious for four or five days. They were all frightened and prayed for him. Ephraim always stood at his bedside. He had forgotten the routine of eating. He would eat a little only if someone pressed him and would rush back to the Vicar's bedside, deeply worried, wondering if the Father had recovered consciousness and had called him while he was away. In those few days, Ephraim became as emaciated as the patient. The Vicar opened his eyes at noon on the fifth day. Ephraim stood there in unrelieved sorrow. The Father opened his eyes from his prolonged sleep and smiled gratefully at him. And Ephraim, recalling that smile later, said to others, 'I will never, ever forget that moment.' A sense of inexpressible awe and joy filled his heart. He knelt down and praised God at length. He bathed himself and had supper for the first time in five days.

None of the parishioners questioned Ephraim's claim that it was his prayer that eventually healed the Father. When one day, postman Peter attempted to contest his claim, how angry the old man became!

It was a week later, when Philipos reached the hills, searching for him, that Thoma heard about the Vicar's illness. Leaving Sara's house, unable to confront Philipos's mother, Thoma had gone straight to his property in the hills.

His land in the hills lay close to the forest. Some of the parishioners maintained that most of that property was encroached forest land, illegally occupied. They hoped the approaching survey of the forest department would reveal the truth. In Thoma's eyes, they were just jealous. It was true that several of them—Mampallyil Anthrayos, Muthukattil Chacko, Thadathil Varghese—wanted to buy that land. But Thoma would not sell it. That may have been why some of them pinned their hopes on the coming forest survey.

Philipos guessed that Thoma would be in the hills. His mother had told him everything. Keeping it to himself, he searched for Thoma to verify the truth. Nobody knew where Thoma was. When he enquired of Yohannan, the boy avoided him, as if he did not hear. So Philipos decided to go and look in the hills. But before he could go, he got busy with other things. He had to go twice or thrice to the town. Then there was the Vicar's illness. And household matters—

'What an idea! You are hiding here, aren't you?' shouted Philipos, as he approached Thoma.

Thoma was scared. Even after he recognized Philipos, it took him some time to steady his heartbeat.

'Who says I am hiding? Hooom, what should I hide for?' Thoma said, struggling to hide his panic.

'Didn't I say it just for fun?' said Philipos.

He was convinced Thoma was scared.

'I came here to see how the cassava was growing,' said Thoma.

'All right, but you didn't tell anyone, did you?'

'I thought about it and I came. What is so important in this to inform the public?' Thoma said with displeasure.

'If you feel that way about it, forget it. What else can I say?'

Philipos sat on the veranda. When Thoma enquired about the parish news, he mentioned the Vicar's illness.

'O, I didn't know that,' Thoma said with a feeling of guilt.

When he saw Philipos looking about, as if searching for something, Thoma went to the room and returned with a bottle of arrack and some cooked rabbit meat. Philipos beamed in satisfaction.

'Altogether, life here is excellent. You don't feel like leaving the hill and going down to the village,' said Thoma.

'Yes, yes.'

When the arrack was almost finished, Philipos deliberately began to speak about Sara. Thoma became pale.

'See, this is what my mother told me.' Starting with this innocent introduction, Philipos sought an explanation from Thoma for being found in suspicious circumstances at Sara's house. Philipos cleverly left out the fact that his mother had insulted and abused Thoma. Sosamma*chedathi* had said to her son that Thoma had been to Sara's house with an ulterior motive. In short, whatever Thoma feared had happened.

He lay on the floor with a deep sigh. Then he gave his friend a full account of everything that happened on that accursed morning. Philipos's face became filled with pity.

'Is it only this much? If this is all, why do you sit depressed as if the flood is coming? That is what I don't understand. The tongue of that mother of mine is a peculiar one—I've known it for a long time. It will never rest idle. Let it go. The word of that vain drunkard Peter is the only evidence against your son. Peter is a dishonest rogue, who enjoys raking up issues embarrassing to others. There is not even a tinge of goodness left in him. He might have made several attempts at Sara's house, after her husband died. He might have gone away rebuffed and abused. Yes, I remember mother saying something like that. I didn't pay attention then. Probably he is taking revenge on Sara by cooking up a story like this. Yes, no doubt. He is a mischief-maker. I know him very well.'

Thoma listened eagerly. He did not distrust Philipos's words. He felt unbearable self-contempt and shame for having tried to accuse a hapless, lonely woman on the basis of an unjust calumny.

'I am sure of one thing,' Philipos continued gravely. 'You won't find a woman as good as Sara in the whole parish. I don't know (he smiled) about other parishes. You see, not only in character (lowering his voice), but in beauty too.'

Thoma sat up and listened.

'Though she has such a good character and exquisite beauty, I doubt there will be a good life for her anymore.'

'Why?' Thoma blurted.

'So it seems to me,' Philipos said with grief. Suddenly he turned toward Thoma, as if urged by some deep impulse from within. 'Can you marry her?'

Thoma was stunned.

'What are you saying?' he asked, his voice raised in distress. But Philipos did not waver.

'I said it after careful consideration.'

'Careful consideration?'

'Yes.'

Philipos began to discuss it in detail. He did not consider age a hindrance against Thoma's marrying Sara. Thoma was around fifty. Sara was about thirty. As it was the second marriage for both, the difference in age could be overlooked. (Philipos completely ignored Thoma's impatient attempt to say something.) There was not the least prospect of a good proposal ever coming for Sara. 'She is a very stubborn woman. Moreover, the death of one's husband, though due to illness, is not something that adds to the esteem of a woman. It is true that he died from illness. However, most of them believe that she has her share of bad luck too. She cannot hope for anyone other than a widower. No one will marry her for wealth, as she has no property other than the small homestead. Also important is the question, how long she will put up with this state of uncertainty. Can good-minded people shirk their duty to save her from this predicament?'

Philipos went on with his analysis, oblivious to Thoma's reaction. As for Yohannan's thoughts and feelings, who knew what the boy would think about his father getting married again? 'He will not oppose it, because he too needs a woman in the house to cook and serve, to sweep the courtyard, and to wash their clothes. It will take at least seven or eight years for him to bring home a woman so capable. He is barely seventeen. At this age, he may feel infatuation for girls, perhaps more than one feels at a more mature age. But boys of this age do not have the courage to consummate their desires on the bodies of girls. They will instead seek another way. It is a way familiar to all, a way less harmful and more convenient. There is nothing to blame them for. They will never dare go into anything requiring considerable effort, I'm sure. Ngh-a, let it go. What matters is we need a woman in the house. Thoma too should desire it. It is a great thing to live knowing the body and mind of a woman instead of the stunted life you are leading now. Why can't Thoma raise himself to the level of desiring Sara…?'

Philipos felt he couldn't help saying one more thing, even though Thoma would call him shameless. It concerned the darkest and most secretive corner of his heart—had Thoma ever slept with a woman after Theresa died? Didn't he ever feel the desire for it afterwards? Don't women ever beckon him in his dreams?

Philipos was unable to believe that a man's feelings die with the death of his wife. Ordinary people can in no way follow the careful observances and sacred discipline of the prophets and saints. Isn't it a sin to ejaculate unknowingly during sleep?

The vision of a green pasture relinquished in the past appeared before Thoma like a divine miracle. Somebody lifted him off his feet and threw him onto it. He fell on his face into the deep lush green. He doesn't feel any pain, it is so wonderful. He feels gooseflesh as the wet grass touches him on his face, ears, hair, and chest. Thoma sat emotionally charged, his eyes fixed on the distant horizon. Darkness began to drop among the trees. Sounds peculiar to the forest begin to be heard. Are the trees speaking to each other?

Philipos placed his hand on his shoulder. 'Didn't you hear all I said?'

'Hmm.'

'This "hmm" is not enough. You must tell me your decision.'

'Decision…?'

'Yes.'

'What decision?'

'Am I to say that?'

'I don't know.'

'Then do one thing.'

'Yes?'

'Give me your word that you will obey what I say.'

'How is that?

'I'll do the rest.'

'But…'

'There is no "but". You have a baseless fear…whether she will consent. I explained all its aspects to you.' He dug his finger painfully into Thoma's shoulder. 'She will consent, a hundred times, sure. Don't worry about it.'

Thoma was scared. He looked at Philipos, bewildered. Philipos burst into a giggle, as if everything was easy and simple. At last, Thoma also joined him.

Thoma and Philipos set out when it dawned very bright. Philipos wanted to leave at night, but Thoma held him back. It was a rare opportunity to drink with a friend. How fortunate we are, when we think of it! Thoma went and came back with more arrack. They drank and talked until midnight. Yet, there was no sleepiness or fatigue on their faces in the morning. Philipos said this to Thoma as they went downhill. The two of them walked toward the valley, laughing. The hill and the sunlight appeared as great blessings to Thoma. The sky was unusually sunny.

'Drop in at our house before you go,' Philipos said. But Thoma was not ready. He was afraid to face Sosamma*chedathi*. But he gave another excuse: 'I must visit the Father. So many days have passed.'

That was the right thing to do, Philipos thought.

'Then, see you tomorrow,' Philipos said with a suggestive look.

'Hmm, tomorrow.'

'Possibly I will even speak to Sara today.'

Thoma smiled with his head down. Philipos gave him a punch on his back.

'There is scope for a big celebration. Don't forget. Let us have it after everything is settled. No hurry. You may go now.'

Though Thoma swung his fist, Philipos cleverly dodged him. Philipos's resounding laughter chased Thoma for some distance. Thoma, too, was smiling to himself. His eyes glittered like stars. Peter was coming from the opposite direction, happily dangling a black cat. Thoma saw him only when he was too near to avoid him.

'O, isn't it Thoma*chettan*? You were nowhere here for a few days. You were in the hills, I suppose.'

'Yes.'

'Why this unusual trip to the hills?'

'No reason.'

'There must have been some reason.'

'I heard wild boars ruined the cultivation and went to check,' Thoma boldly lied. Peter twitched his cheeks as usual. The cat lamented. Its last supper was already over.

'Are there no letters today?'

He only meant to be friendly.

'No letters. I'm on leave today.'

Peter lifted up the cat. He examined it. It must have guessed by now what kind of person he was and what secret purpose he was nursing. There was distress on its face.

'I'm going,' said Thoma. He was in a hurry. A pig and her two piglets trotted along his path. Thoma remembered the empty pigsty at home. He recalled with loss and grief that it was once full of pigs. They used to wander in the compound all the time, grunting from dawn to dusk. Every one of them was lost. Hmm, never mind. We will raise pigs again, Thoma decided. More pigs than we ever had. The sty will be filled with piglets. We will build more cages. We will raise poultry, ducks, and rabbits. We also need a good dog. And all along the boundary, we will plant pineapple, guava, jambu, and suppota.

With a full heart, Thoma walked on with quick, long steps. Then he, he alone, heard a song of praise to God. It fell on his ears and passed him like a blowing wind. He did not disbelieve it. He would recite every word of it if anyone asked him. The hymn was so vivid to him. When he raised his head, wondering at how marvelous it was, he saw the doves. They circled above the church, flapping their wings, but not going far. All the while he spent in the Vicar's room, Thoma could hear them. Sitting on the tiled roof, they cooed and flapped their wings.

The visit was very short. Thoma stood there some time looking unblinkingly at the Vicar. The priest was in a condition to speak no more than two words. It was the guilt and distress he felt when he saw the profound sorrow in the priest's eyes that made him wish to leave so quickly. When Thoma sadly said that he was leaving, the priest moved his head a little. Thoma felt great relief, when he came out. Behind him came Ephraim. He asked where Thoma had been for the past few days. He did not expect a reply and hurried back to the Vicar's room, as if he had fulfilled his mission. Thoma felt extremely bad. The doves went on cooing and rustling. Thoma stood some time waiting for Ephraim, but he did not see him again. He wondered what Ephraim's behaviour really meant. Perhaps Ephraim suddenly remembered some medicine he had forgotten to give to the Father. Thoma consoled himself with this thought and went home. On the way, he came across several acquaintances. Some of them asked him to explain his absence. Thoma satisfied them. They got into other matters concerning the parish. They talked about making a road and extending the bus service by building a concrete bridge across the river in place of the suspension bridge. Thoma felt there was widespread optimism among the people. No one seemed depressed and helpless. What they had, instead, were faith and hope. Their faces clearly announced there was no place for disappointment. Thoma was pleased.

It was nearly noon when he reached home. Yohannan was on the veranda. As soon as he saw his father, he disappeared into the house. Thoma did not fail to notice it. He removed his sandals, shirt, and vest, and sat on the coir bed. It was the beginning of pleasing thoughts. He heard pots clinking inside, but he had no appetite. He surveyed his own body. He caressed his stomach. He massaged his left hand with his right hand. There was no loosening of the skin or the flesh. (That was not perfectly true.) He lighted a beedi. Halfway through it, he tossed it out. His eyelids drooped. He stretched his arms and body and took a deep breath. Letting out a yawn, he lay down on his back. Before long he fell asleep.

He slept until 4 in the afternoon. He lay still for half an hour after waking. His mind wandered confused, as if confronted by a crossword puzzle. It wandered after every hint. It wandered in search of meaning, in search of words, trying to fill in the blanks...and finally became tired. He walked out and felt the breeze. His weariness left him as he dipped himself in the river. He felt an urge to swim, but it seemed he had almost forgotten how to swim. He suddenly began to pant for breath. When he looked toward the bank, he saw two children standing there. They were laughing at his awkward swimming. Taking it as a challenge, he went to the other bank one more time and came back. A boy shouted, 'Once more!' Thoma smiled a happy, sunny smile. How naughty! When he splashed water at them, they dodged him, laughing aloud. Thoma beckoned them into the river. 'No, we won't come,' replied the girl. Her voice was like the soft jingle of the bell. 'Where are you from?' Thoma called out to them. 'We belong to this place here,' said the girl. The two of them ran away without waiting to say anything. Thoma wanted to speak to them for a little longer, but they were nowhere to be seen. They must have gone home.

Thoma rubbed his body briskly. He ought to have bathed with soap, he thought. He decided to buy some. Soap was considered necessary for bathing when he was young. Gradually the habit changed. Bathing without soap became a matter of no concern. Later, the very thought of soap was forgotten… The smell of certain kinds of soap persisted for hours. What was the soap that Theresa used? Its name…it is at the tip of my tongue. Hmm, let it go. Several times he dipped in the river and rose. Then, standing in the water, he took off the towel, wrung it out, and began to wipe his head and body dry with it. Then he heard a mocking voice: 'Hey!' It was that boy. He disappeared after making the sound. Thoma giggled. So did the river. A wind blew on the trees.

He dressed at home and went out walking again. He came across Philipos near Lohitakshan's barbershop. Philipos was making fun of Lohitakshan, pointing out some of his eccentric frailties. Lohitakshan was not in the least interested in women. What he wanted was porn books and nude erotic illustrations of sex. Thoma stood for a while listening to Philipos making fun of Lohitakshan. Bored of it, he said, 'Ngh-a, enough, leave him alone.' He put his hand on Philipos's shoulder and took him along on his walk. Thoma was too diffident to ask him about Sara. Philipos spoke warily. He talked of many other things. Thoma did not show interest in them. Philipos brought to his notice a press report of the manifestation of Christ's figure in a church in some province. Finding him uninterested in that also, he finally said, 'That other matter seems almost settled.'

'What other matter?' Thoma enquired indifferently.

'Don't you know? Let it go, man. Don't try to dodge the subject.'

Thoma smiled. 'Truly, I don't know what you are saying. What can I do, if you speak in such a roundabout way?'

'Then I am washing my hands of it,' said Philipos.

'Give me strength! Say it more clearly. Did you enquire?'

'That's more like it!' Philipos said, rather loudly. Thoma was afraid someone would hear.

'Come let's have a drink…on me.'

Philipos led Thoma by the hand. Thoma did not want to drink, but it was Philipos who was inviting him. They sat aside in a corner, drinking arrack.

Philipos said, 'I did not speak to her today. I went there three times to do just that, but her sister Katrina is there visiting. She will leave tomorrow. I could speak to Katrina or her husband, but that won't do. Her consent is the problem. We need to get that first. Don't worry about it. Let's do it tomorrow.'

Thoma sat quite indifferently, as if thinking about something else. In his heart, he was unable to feel displeasure at Philipos. As they parted, Philipos said, 'I'll come most probably tomorrow morning. You must be at home.'

'Come whenever you can. I'll be at home.'

Thoma turned to his road. It was dark everywhere. Darkness greeted the wayfarer. It embraced him. Thoma did not feel bad about it. He wholeheartedly submitted to it. When he got home, he lay down as usual on his back, his hands tucked under his head, anxiously pondering the possible consequences. He smiled at the thought of Sara. In his remembrance, Sara came like a honeyed word. She had become the most beautiful, fed on lean flour, oil, and honey. Biting her lower lip, suppressing a smile suggestive of pleasure and desire, and her body uncovered, Sara slowly held out her hand. Her fingers trembled.

Behold, when he said to her, 'God is witness between you and me,' she said to him, 'I'm here.' He lay with his mouth upon her mouth, his eyes upon her eyes, and his palms upon her palms.

Then Thoma woke, and knew it was a dream.

He sat, walked, and smoked. Then, controlling himself, he lay down to sleep again.

When he slept again, he wandered, searching for someone in a valley where snow was falling, trees were shedding leaves, and it was blowing cold. He did not know what time of day or night it was. There was a half-light all around him. He was not sure whether it was just before nightfall or immediately after night. Leaves and snow kept falling on his body.

That night's sleep seemed to Thoma like walking blind. Trudging with cautious steps, he would suddenly stumble on something. Sometimes, it was a tree of thorns, or a huge fish dangling from a tree, or a bowl of wine, or a long cloak drying on the clothes line, or loose, flowing hair, or breasts… he walked on, occasionally losing his temper at all the bad things he saw. Certain things he could not make out, he touched them so briefly. When he stretched out his fingers once again to touch them, those tantalizing things moved farther and farther away.

What an awful night! Thoma tossed and turned. The bed did not like it. 'Lie still,' it rebuked him. Thoma would not obey. 'Look, right now I will break down and fall to pieces on the floor,' the bed lamented… Thoma apologized to it and lay quite still. But not for long. It was such an awful night. Thoma, that night, was a quite different Thoma. The craving for Sara's seductive body burned in him. Sometimes, he even fantasized she was with him. Afraid that Sara was leaving his tent, he was going to cry aloud. He felt someone was performing witchcraft against him. Warding it off with the power of his will, he took Sara in his arms. He held her slim, hot body close to him, with a flush of passion. He frantically babbled something in her ears. He ejaculated thrice. It was such an exciting night. A strange night! In the course of the night, it became bright—brighter than day—and more cheerful. But nowhere was the sun visible. A white sky stood bright and full, as if boundlessly benevolent. Suddenly the night became dark, darker and bleaker than any other night.

Thoma feared he was going mad.

'Lord, give me Sara, not madness,' he prayed eagerly. He waved the censer before every idol of the holy saints. The doves flapped their wings in the fragrant fumes.

Words flapped wings inside Thoma. He recovered all those words forgotten during his careless, disorderly days. 'My darling, my beautiful, my delight...' He ran around gathering flowers and showered them at her feet...my sweetheart, my darling dove...He clasped her tightly. He took her lips into his mouth and squeezed them like a honeycomb. Taking her in his arms he walked toward the river. She laughed aloud and softly hit him on his back.

My God, what an awful night this is! Thoma woke panting and was fairly bewildered. Yet he prayed for the night never to end. It was such a splendid night.

It was near daybreak that he enjoyed some uninterrupted sleep. So, he did not know when the morning came.

When Yohannan came out and looked, Thoma was in deep sleep. He slept as peacefully and innocently as a child.

Leaving him to sleep, Yohannan walked toward the river. Thoma never knew he had gone.

He woke up an hour later. O, he looked all about quite bewildered. The night has ended. It is very late. Perhaps the day is about to end.

Thoma leaped to his feet. His steps faltered. Why this hurry, he thought. His heart was writhing. Blood flooded through his veins. My God, my God! He prayed silently. Then he eagerly got ready for the day.

By about noon, Thoma had taken an important decision, to go and meet Sara in the evening.

He lost patience waiting for Philipos to come and announce Sara's consent. He distressed himself worrying that either Philipos might not have taken it so seriously or that he might have forgotten it completely, while poking his nose into other distractions in the morning. He cursed Philipos. If only Philipos knew how afflicted he had been last night! If only he knew a fraction of it! The question Philipos posed yesterday as to why Thoma couldn't raise himself to the level of desiring Sara filled his mind like a revelation.

Philipos, behold, I have raised myself to the level you wanted me to reach. Place your hand on my chest to feel who I have become overnight and how far I have raised myself to the desired level. Feel the writhing of my soul... Until yesterday, Thoma may have been an unclean person. The Thoma, who went about lazily without cutting his nails, without scrubbing the dirt off his feet, without shaving properly and regularly, and wearing a shirt stinking of sweat, breathed his last yesterday. He has been buried in a corner, where no one will dare to look. His was the death of a pig. Not a single tear fell on his corpse. Now look. Here is a Thoma who is saintly. He has cut his nails, washed his feet clean, shaved his face, removed the grey hairs from his moustache and plucked the hairs protruding from his nose. This shirt does not stink of sweat. It has long been kept washed and pressed. It even smells of freshness. This festival dress has been lying idle. I have taken it out for another festival. 'My patient endurance has finally borne fruit,' says the shirt gladly. Those damn hairs growing thick in the nostrils were a nuisance. How nice it is today, says the nose. The feet feel proud of their clean toes and heels. The cheeks laugh. The body kisses the shirt, as if it were a baby. There is a bustle altogether. But Philipos is late. No, he is not likely to forget. He has the sincerity of heart to understand how important and decisive the matter is. He is a good fellow. Wait! Be grateful to him. Killing a fatted calf, he will appear any time with Sara's message. Shall I visit Sara in the evening alone? No. Take Philipos along. He must be there to chalk out the details. Or that can be done tomorrow. Today I will go alone to see her. I may be able to tell her about last night, if I get words. How will she take it? I must tell her everything no matter what she feels. I must tell her everything that has happened to me in life till today. It may take several days and nights. At intervals, I will kiss her.

Her lips, though slightly pale, are charming. She will caress my chest. My God, where have you detained that Philipos? Send him here hastily; yes, send him very hastily.

Philipos arrived before long. As soon as he saw Philipos at a distance, Thoma controlled himself and lay down on the bed pretending to sleep. The leaves rustled in the wind. Then he heard the approaching footsteps. Thoma's heart began to beat faster. When Philipos touched him and called, he woke laboriously, as if climbing up from the bottomless deep.

'O, it is you,' he said indifferently, lighting a beedi. He offered one to Philipos too.

But his body trembled. Hiding his eagerness, he sat waiting for Philipos to open his mouth. They were unusual moments of self-control. Taking a vigorous puff of the beedi, Thoma observed that Philipos also seemed to be thinking something.

Suddenly Philipos said with a resounding laugh, 'Hooom, never mind! We'll find another match. It is not very difficult, is it?'

Thoma gaped at Philipos without understanding what he was saying. Philipos said light-heartedly, 'She says she is marrying no one. Hoom, she is unwisely turning down an excellent proposal. She will certainly regret it, today or tomorrow.'

It was then he noticed that Thoma looked thunderstruck.

'Ha!' He slapped Thoma on the shoulder and said, 'But why do you sit gaping like this? I will arrange a good match for you in two days. Let her go to hell. Is she eyeing someone else? I don't know. Anyway, I've decided I must keep an eye on her from now on. Ha! What happened to you?'

Like a dying man taking his last view of the earth, Thoma looked at Philipos.

'What did she say?' He enquired in a subdued trembling voice.

Philipos became worried. He was a bit confused.

'I met her early this morning. I told her the matter bluntly. She says she is marrying no one. I tried to counsel her a little. But—'

'Go away.' Thoma waved his hand at Philipos.

Philipos was utterly amazed at the change of expression on Thoma's face. He rose to his feet, stood there hesitating for a while, and slowly walked away. He turned and looked back several times before he reached the road, but he did not see Thoma.

Thoma sat stiff and benumbed. His eyes were fixed on a distant empty space. Birds sitting on the wall cast their droppings into his vision. But he was unable to see it. He began to sob in bitterness. His heart ached as if hit by a blow. It was a fierce ache. Lying on his left side and thinking of his great sorrow, he wept. And thus it became a house of mourning. Dust fell from its walls and pillars. The house looked at its master, who was sobbing, helpless, and humiliated. The house looked at him, wondering what he would do. What will he do?

Thoma took obscure paths, concealing himself like a thief or an adulterer. He passed by the field of a lazy man and by the vineyard of a stupid person. He saw it was all overgrown with thorns and the ground was covered with nettles. And its stone wall was broken down.

He saw the sky was perturbed.

Thoma walked, crying and shuddering like a person destined to fear the whole world without any reason. At the same time, at intervals there appeared on his face a fleeting hope that a way out would somehow open up.

Yes, he was going to meet Sara. After he heard Sara's decision from Philipos, he lay on the bed crying bitterly, forgetting everything. He lay there receiving sympathy from the walls of the house and everything around him. He could see only one house then. It was Sara's house.

Sara, I come looking at your house, crying and trembling. I am perplexed not by darkness. Nor am I worried by the darkness covering my face.

To avoid meeting people, he shunned all the main roads and made his way through deserted properties, meadows, and woods. As he walked stealthily, unseen and unheard, suddenly he heard something like an ominous sound foreboding danger. When he turned and looked, he saw a tree falling.

Thoma was startled. There was not even a light wind blowing. The tree fell slowly, taking some time to pull out its roots from the earth. The mystery of that accidental tragedy drenched his chest and face in sweat. His palms burned like fire.

Suddenly he felt his heart trembling and shifting from its place. He became anxious that he would fall down dead, before he reached Sara's house. Still he struggled on.

Sara, Sara, I'm not yet dead and gone, thanks to the grace of the Almighty. Then from behind, he heard mocking laughter with a thousand sharp points. Ha...Ha...Ha... It was the laughter of the devil. Standing close to a rock the devil laughed at him.

'O, Jesus!' he cried and ran away frightened, using all his strength.

He stopped puffing and panting in an open clearing and looked back. He let out a sigh. There was no sign of the devil. He felt great relief. Yes, he tried to convince himself. The devil can neither prevent nor dissuade me from meeting Sara. Demons do not have so much strength. They have never had the power to defeat man. Man will love and trust his fellow man. He will raise his spirit. Look at this Thoma, who desired Sara.

Sara, I will tell you everything. I will tell you about a girl on a holy Christmas evening, a secret guarded in the safest corner of the mind, a secret never revealed even in the weakest moments of confession... I will tell you about my Fridays and Sundays, about my night dreams. I will tell you all, all... But before that, give your heart to me, Sara. We will share the experience of peaceful joy.

Thoma remembered something and smiled to himself. It was a short-lived cheer. He thought how deplorable it would be, if Philipos were right about Sara's stubbornness. At the same time, he felt the hope that he would be able to persuade her and lead her to the right path of life.

Sara, you are beautiful. But don't you know a beautiful woman without wisdom is like a golden nose-ring in a swine's nose. Wisdom is better than silver. The quietness of the tongue is the tree of life. Its crookedness is sorrow of mind. You remember the proverbs. A virtuous woman is more precious than rubies. The heart of her husband trusts in her. He will have no need of spoils. She does him good, and not harm, all the days of her life. She seeks wool and flax, and works with willing hands. She is like the merchants' ships; she brings food from far away. She rises early in the morning and provides food for her household and a share for her servant girls. She considers a field and buys it. With the fruits of her hands, she plants a vineyard. She girds herself with strength and makes her arms strong. She perceives that her merchandise is profitable. Her lamp does not go out at night. She lays her hands to the spindle and her hands hold the distaff. She opens her hands to the poor, yes, she reaches out her hands to the needy. She is not afraid of the cold, because all her household have blankets of wool. Her children rise up and call her blessed. Her husband praises her. Many women have done excellently; but you surpass them all.

Thoma walked panting through the dry, lazy afternoon, through the yawning sounds of trees, through the afternoon nap of the stones, through the sunlight, which does not know if it has a father.

A house leaning toward life is Sara's house. Its door was shut.

Sweat was streaming into his eyes. He looked all around him. Where is Sara? What does the closed door mean?

In his heart, the call 'Sara, Sara' rose louder and louder. He faltered and lost his balance. He held tight to the pillar.

Then he heard voices from the room; a laugh, like water came flowing to where he stood.

Thoma ran toward the door like a mad man. Then he retreated without banging on the door. Let Sara be happy. Let her know love. He controlled himself and came out of the veranda. He walked two steps with the feeling of a card player returning after losing his last coin. Sara laughed again. Who might be with her? Who might be the person she knows love from?

He walked toward the back of the house. In the wall of burnt bricks, he saw a window with wooden bars. He sidled to the window and peeped into the room.

In the room were Yohannan and Sara. Sitting on the coir bed, Yohannan tried a cigarette. From the reed mat spread on the floor, Sara smiled at him. Yohannan saw Sara through the smoke. He saw her breasts heaving and the creases on her stomach quivering. Then she said to him, 'I have refused your father.'

'Well done.' Yohannan nodded his head. 'Father must have turned pale, when he heard it.'

'Yes.'

'I have no regrets.'

'Neither do I.'

Yohannan looked at the smoke for a little while.

'Is what we do a sin?'

Sara had no answer for that. Yohannan, disappointed, nodded his head and said, 'I don't know either. We cannot expect an answer for every question.'

Yohannan sat leaning against the wall. Throwing away the dying cigarette, he looked at Sara. He said, 'Finally, you are the only one I have. Is it not by God's grace that we have at last united like this, after moving away from everyone else and wandering along hundreds of pathways? I feel that way. I may be wrong. But now I think, I love God. Sara, what do you think?'

Sara lifted her glistening, oily face toward him. The scent of frankincense spread in the room. It truly amazed Sara.

'Nobody has burnt frankincense here. But the scent of frankincense is spreading,' she said.

'Yes, I too smell frankincense,' said Yohannan.

He puzzled over it.

Sara said, 'I'm sure you brought it.'

Yohannan smiled. 'Your mouth speaks the truth.'

Then she held her hand out to him. He went near her and they sat hand in hand.

'Sara!'

'Yes.'

'Your eyes are like doves. Your hair is like a flock of goats. Your teeth are like a flock of shorn ewes coming up from the washing. Your lips are like a crimson thread.'

He kissed her. She said, 'Your mouth is sweet. You are like a lemon tree among the trees of the wood. Your eyes are bathed in milk. Your cheeks are spices.'

They fell into each other's arms. Her hair touched his face.

'How fragrant is the scent of your oil!' he said.

'How sweet is your love!' she said.

He smelled her clothes and ran his fingers through her hair and neck. He bared her breasts, caressed them and said, 'Your breasts are like bunches of grapes.'

He pressed his face, which shone like a word of kindness, between her breasts. She lay with her eyes closed.

'My love, my dove…' His voice grew tender. His touch became more intense. The wind blew on the leaves of the tree of life.

Thoma stood stupefied with his back against the wall. He could hear everything. Each word racked him. He would have fallen down but for the wall. His body and face were drenched in sweat. The wind was blowing, but it could not dry him.

In front of him lay the vast expanse of greenery. He could see the forest at a distance and he saw the sky above it.

When he turned his eyes toward the valley, the valley sympathized with him. The wood and the sky also commiserated with him. Poor Thoma, poor…

Exhausted, he sat on the ground. His soul sobbed wildly.

The earth and the wall looked at each other wondering how to console him.

There is a time for everything, and a season for every purpose under heaven: a time to be born, and a time to die…a time to break down, and a time to build up…a time to mourn, and a time to dance…a time to embrace, and a time to refrain from embracing…a time to love, and a time to hate.

Yes, everything has a time.

Thoma gaped. He was quite perplexed and looked pale and drawn, like a man who wakes from a long coma. He felt he had been sitting there for numberless years. How many floods, tempests, famines, and hailstorms have come and gone. How many towers have been raised and have fallen. Men have gathered and dispersed. How many treaties were signed and promises made. There were births and deaths…what were all the things that happened… dreams, imprisonments, days of mourning, benedictions, prophecies, times of exodus, torture, plagues, darkness, feasts, the Passover, the commandments, tents, vestments, censers, revelations, the tablet of heart, sacrifice…

Having come round, Thoma rose to his feet. With heaving sighs and faltering steps, he came to the front of the house. He looked toward the door, which was open now.

He climbed to the veranda. Crossing the threshold, he reached the room where Sara lay asleep.

He saw all these things. Her clothes were white. She had her left leg raised close to the wall. Her loose hair was scattered. Her left hand lay across her chest. Her right hand stretched to the floor. Sweat glistened on her skin. Upon her lips was the light of a tender smile. Over her closed eyes was the wetness of tears.

He wondered if there was anyone like Sara. But he thought: Sara too will die. The spirit will return to God. The dust will return to dust as it was long ago. Sara…nothing will remain…this beautiful face, these eyes like the eyes of the dove, the lips sweet as honeycomb, the tongue with milk and honey under it, the neck like an ivory tower, breasts like two twin fawns, the belly like a heap of wheat encircled with lilies, a navel like a rounded bowl, and the wine in it.

He stood looking at her with sympathy. Her beauty multiplied ten times, when he linked it with death and degeneration. With a weary smile, he bent down. Sara… His hands went toward her neck.

Thoma was coming out of Sara's house with wavering steps when Sosamma*chedathi* and Brigithamma arrived.

They were stunned, when they saw him. He looked at them quite indifferently and went away down the slope.

Sosamma*chedathi* stood creasing her forehead in anger. Brigithamma went to look for Sara, and Sosamma*chedathi* turned back to go with her into Sara's room.

Sara did not see them. She did not hear when they called her. Blood flowed from the left corner of her mouth.

Yohannan looked at the earth and found it formless and void. He looked at the sky; it had no light. He looked at the mountains, and found them quaking. All the hills were shaking. All the birds in the sky had flown away.

Yohannan stood on the earth, which was formless and void, and under a sky, which was without light.

As he walked with a heavy, painful heart, David sang a hymn to the leader of the choir, with stringed instruments according to the eighth raga.

I am so exhausted by my grief; every night, I flood my bed with tears; I drench my couch with my weeping. My eyes waste away because of grief; they grow weak because of all my foes. Depart from me, all you workers of evil.

Yohannan sat at the feet of the Vicar. Hide me under the shadow of your wings, he said to himself.

Outside the door were trees with shrivelled leaves, open graves, and fire.

The Father pressed his shivering palm upon Yohannan's head.

'May God desist from cursing us.' Yohannan saw the Father's pale lips tremble.

He again called out from the deep that had swallowed him. 'May God desist from cursing us.'

After this, he rose from his chair, moved to a corner, knelt down and began to pray. Yohannan watched him indifferently for a little while and then walked toward the door.

Ephraim was standing outside. The agony of the evil days was reflected in his eyes. He moved his lips to say something to Yohannan. But Yohannan could not hear anything. As his feet touched the sand in the courtyard, his eyes turned toward the canopy of sky above the church cross. There was light. There were birds. The light was huge. The birds were flying. Yohannan looked up and saw the cemetery. There were trees of mourning planted and watered by the spirits. A wind passed through them. He felt his eyes were filled with tears. He put on sorrow like a cloak and walked.

'Esther!' Daniel called out aloud. Esther came out.

Seeing Yohannan with Daniel, she ran toward him in amazement.

'Come, son. How long it has been since I saw you!' She took his hand. Esther's heart sorrowed looking at his face. She led him to the veranda. 'Son, please sit.'

'I found him on the road,' said Daniel. He saw him wandering like an orphan, harassed and suffering.

Esther looked him up and down. 'Son, you have become so thin. You also look tired.'

Valsamma came running from somewhere in the compound. The dog followed her. She had probably been playing with it.

'Give something to eat. I am hungry,' said Daniel.

'I will serve food just now.' Taking Agnes with her, Esther went inside. A little while later, Agnes brought water for washing their hands. She smiled sadly at Yohannan. Yohannan did not see it. Susan came and stood at the door. Her face also was sympathetic.

'Son, wash your hands,' Daniel said.

He obeyed. He took the water to the courtyard and came back with his hands washed. Utterly distressed, Esther and her daughters watched him sitting by Daniel's side and silently eating his rice.

Yohannan saw them, when he raised his face, and suddenly dropped his head. He had a lump in his throat and found it hard to breathe. He drank the glass of jeera water in one long gulp. He looked at Daniel to imply he had finished with his meal.

'Why, the rice is almost untouched! Give him some more fish,' Daniel said in a panic. Esther hurried over with the bowl of fish curry.

'No.'

'Son, why?' asked Esther.

'No.'

'A little fried vegetable?'

'No, I am full.'

Esther straightened herself up.

'Do you cook anything at home?'

'Yes.'

'I don't think he cooks. Look, how thin he has become!'

Yohannan did not say anything. He sat looking at his plate.

'Son, do one thing. Stay with us here. Joshi will be happy.' Yohannan looked at Esther bewildered. Then he dropped his face without saying anything. Esther thought, he did not like the idea. Worriedly, she turned to Daniel.

Daniel said, 'Don't stay there alone. If you're alone and idle, your mind will have the chance to house troublesome thoughts. Here you have company. The children will consider you as their elder brother. And we will regard you as our own son.'

Esther said, 'Son, you can live here, like our Joshi.'

'But—' Yohannan stopped abruptly and rose to his feet. At the door, he turned and looked. Everybody was sad. He came out. He washed his hands and sat in the veranda, turning the pages of Susan's biology text. Daniel sat a little away from him, fixing his eyes on the floor. Behind him was Esther.

'Yesterday, we had a letter from Joshi,' Esther informed him.

Yohannan looked up.

'There is nothing in particular. He is well. Ngh-a, then, you didn't reply to his two or three letters, did you?'

Yohannan remembered Joshi. Joshi... Joshi... May he come down, like the rain that falls on the mown grass, and like showers that water the earth... May the time come, when people will bless each other calling his name... I am wretched and poor...I go away like a passing shadow.

There was sunlight on the way. But Yohannan did not try to cover himself. His forehead was covered in sweat. But he did not bother to wipe it. His eyes fell on the distant forest. The forest stood like a wall.

He walked with his head down. Brigithamma came upon him, near a bamboo clump. He did not see her coming toward him. When he passed her, she turned and looked at him. Simultaneously, Yohannan also turned, thinking he had heard some sound. Brigithamma covered her mouth, as if to hold back a heaving sob.

The tufts of bamboos swayed above them.

Yohannan started walking again. Brigithamma stood beneath the bamboos remembering several things past. Yohannan did not remember anything. He walked lightly, without feeling the smallest burden on his chest.

At one place on the road, Yohannan came upon a man who was sleeping with his face buried in the grass. Yielding to some inner impulse, Yohannan went near him. He sat in the grass and bent his head. He tapped the sleeper on the back and called him.

The sleeper woke, raised his face from the grass, and turned toward him. It was Yakob.

Yohannan was not frightened.

'Are you sleeping?' he asked.

'Yes,' Yakob growled and again hid his face in the lush green grass. Yohannan slowly rose to his feet and walked away.

A familiar river…birds inhabit and sing along the banks… little lambs frolic there. Yes, they frolic…

Yohannan stood still, taking in the view. As they moved away to the dark rocks and bushes, he started walking again.

A welcoming footpath runs through the dense cluster of grass, flattening the blades.

He stopped suddenly and looked across the grass.

A little behind him were two children—a boy and a girl.

They stood watching him carefully. But he did not see them.

He stooped and searched desperately for Rahel in the grass. Unable to find her there, he walked on and looked around wondering where else she could be. Then he saw the children and hurried away, intent on escaping them.

The river lay to his left. The water was still. There was no echoing sound over it.

Yohannan walked sorrowing.

The house… The doves sat cooing upon the roof. Yohannan said to the gates to lift up their heads and to the ancient doors to be lifted up.

Walking with faltering steps, he reached the veranda. Grandfather was sorrowfully reading the Bible.

'As for mortals, their days are like grass. They flourish like a flower of the field. It is gone when the wind passes over it; and its place knows it no more.'

Grey, wet eyes rise from the Holy Book.

The wind is growling outside.

Yohannan walked to his room. It was almost dark.

The doves were cooing on the roof. Yohannan took his clothes off and sat in the dust on the floor, leaning against the wall, and cried:

'*Ayyo*, O earth, do not cover my blood; do not let my cry be hindered!'

GLOSSARY

achen: Christian priest or father

amma: mother

ayuss: the total number of years of a person's life

ayussinte: of ayuss

chechi: elder sister

chedathi: elderly woman

chettan: elder brother; elderly man

kochachen: assistant priest

pusthakam: book

anjili: a tree used for timber

arishtam: a medicinal drink made of herbs and alcohol

attuvanchi: a tree found along riverbanks

ayyo: an exclamation of surprise, fear or pain

mol: daughter

mon: son

Passover: Some Christians observe a form of the Jewish holiday of Passover. It is often linked to the Christian holiday and festival of Easter. The redemption from the bondage of sin through the sacrifice of Christ is celebrated, a parallel of the Jewish Passover's celebration of redemption from bondage in the land of Egypt.